She was good e... Sheikh Kahlil's child, but not good enough to sit beside him on the throne of Abadan.

But what good would anger do? She wondered, feeling her fury quickly overtaken by despair. For her son's sake she would do this. For her son's sake she would marry the man she loved, and then be humiliated by him after six short months, when he divorced her in front of the entire world.

Lucy looked at Kahlil as if seeing him clearly for the first time. Even now she couldn't hate him. She could only love him. And if six months was all Kahlil had to offer, then she would take six months.

Dear Reader,

I just loved writing this book, with the wide sweep of the desert as a backdrop.

I hope you enjoy reading about Kahlil and Lucy coming together in spite of all the seemingly insurmountable difficulties they must face.

Do drop me a line through my Web site, www.susanstephens.net, and catch up on all the latest writing gossip in my writing diary!

Happy reading, everyone!

Susan

Find rapture in the sands
available only from Harlequin Presents®

Susan Stephens

THE SHEIKH'S CAPTIVE BRIDE

Surrender To
The Sheikh

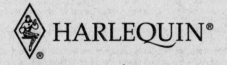

HARLEQUIN®

TORONTO • NEW YORK • LONDON
AMSTERDAM • PARIS • SYDNEY • HAMBURG
STOCKHOLM • ATHENS • TOKYO • MILAN • MADRID
PRAGUE • WARSAW • BUDAPEST • AUCKLAND

For Kate.

ISBN 0-373-12485-6

THE SHEIKH'S CAPTIVE BRIDE

First North American Publication 2005.

Copyright © 2005 by Susan Stephens.

This edition published by arrangement with Harlequin Books S.A.

® and TM are trademarks of the publisher. Trademarks indicated with ® are registered in the United States Patent and Trademark Office, the Canadian Trade Marks Office and in other countries.

www.eHarlequin.com

Printed in U.S.A.

PROLOGUE

THE royal council chamber in the Golden Palace of Abadan was drenched in light as Sheikh Kahlil ben Saeed Al-Sharif indicated his wish to move the meeting on.

'Highness—'

Kahlil's dark gaze switched to the face of his most trusted advisor, Abdul Hassan.

'You have reached a decision regarding your new palace, Majesty?'

Kahlil saw anticipation flare behind the eyes of every man seated with him around the council table. Even amongst such an unimaginably wealthy group the rivalry was intense. Prestigious contracts always held an opportunity for someone. But his decision would disappoint them.

'I shall not be building my new palace in Abadan.' Kahlil allowed the murmurs of disappointment to settle. 'I have identified a village in Europe—and an appropriate residence.' His thoughts flew to the village of Westbury, and the Hall—which he intended to buy. Though there was a problem, small, but irritating none the less, he remembered, thinking of Lucy Benson.

When he'd settled upon Westbury, in amongst the pile of documents sent to help him make his choice he had seen a local magazine that contained the photograph of a young woman. She had a look in her eyes that drew his attention. The caption said Lucy Benson was an interior designer, and, lately, a property developer. And she had bought Westbury Hall, the very property he intended to own. Interior decorator to property developer was a quite a leap. Could she make it?

5

Kahlil's mind drifted towards golden hair tumbling in exuberant waves around a heart-shaped face, and a simple summer dress clinging to voluptuous curves that made him despise the fashion to be thin. Her lips appeared red without artifice, and were parted sufficiently to reveal pearl-white teeth: teeth he could easily imagine nipping his flesh in the throes of passion. Picturing them naked together—Lucy Benson's soft body yielding beneath his hard-muscled frame—called for every bit of his control.

But the camera had captured more than her likeness, Kahlil remembered. Her character was betrayed by the stubborn tilt of her chin, and the look of sheer determination in her midnight-blue eyes. As son of the ruling Sheikh, he had every material possession a man could desire, but he came from a warrior race, a passionate land; challenge was in his blood. And she was an independent woman who would fight him every inch of the way. He could hardly wait. Taming Lucy Benson would be an interesting bonus on top of wresting the Hall from her grasp.

'The village of Westbury is well situated,' he said, turning his attention to the council again. 'It is close to the sea, so we can bring the yacht in, and only a short drive from the airport for the jet. It will be a novelty,' he added, with a closing gesture of his hand.

Everyone understood this, and the tension around the table lifted. For men who had everything, novelty was the most valuable currency of all.

'Westbury is a good choice, Majesty.'

Abdul Hassan spoke for the council, and Kahlil inclined his head in gracious acknowledgement of his approval.

'The village is prosperous and full of character,' Abdul Hassan continued, 'though some areas are in need of improvement.'

'Not all areas,' Kahlil murmured, thinking of Lucy Benson.

'Indeed, Majesty,' Abdul Rachman agreed, dipping his head respectfully. 'How may we assist you further in this matter?'

'Make arrangements for a visit to Westbury,' Kahlil instructed. 'I'm going to make a thorough evaluation of the project for myself.'

CHAPTER ONE

SHE was alone again at last. Linking her hands behind her head, Lucy Benson stared at the ceiling and gave vent to her frustration with a desperate, angry sound. Losing Westbury Hall was awful; facing her creditors was worse. Letting everyone down at the last minute was the hardest thing she had ever had to do. Her plans to renovate the grand old house where she had grown up had collapsed for want of just a little more money. The builders had found some serious and costly structural faults, and then, quite suddenly, the bank had pulled out.

From housekeeper's daughter to owner and developer had been a bit ambitious, Lucy knew, but for a few short months it had seemed achievable. She had risked everything to restore the Hall to its former glory, so that it could become a living tribute to the kindly old lady who had lived there. But she had failed Aunt Grace, Lucy thought as she took a last look around. And that hurt most of all.

She blinked back tears. She couldn't cry, not with sunlight streaming optimistically through the domed stained glass cupola—rain would have been more appropriate. Some of the opposing plans had included knocking the old Hall down. But she couldn't allow the elegant building to be supplanted by a featureless block of modern flats, she just couldn't—

'Excuse me.'

Lucy whirled on her heels, her heart thundering wildly. She had thought she was alone. The male voice was deep and slightly accented, and it took her a moment to see where it was coming from. But then she saw the man standing half cloaked in shadows by the front door. He was tall, and dark, and casually dressed—like most of the other creditors. This was not an occasion for dressing to impress, she thought dryly.

'I didn't mean to frighten you.'

Lucy wasn't convinced. There was something about the man that suggested he was accustomed to using his stature to best advantage; he was far too confident. 'I thought everyone had gone,' she said coolly.

'Am I too late?'

'No, of course not. Come in, and I'll tell you what I told the others.'

'The others?'

'Creditors,' Lucy said, retracing her steps across the black and white marble tiles. 'Please, sit down,' she added, opening the door to her improvised meeting room. There were some hard-backed chairs in the echoing dining room, and she had set up a decorator's table for people to gather around. He followed her into the room. 'Lucy Benson,' Lucy said, turning to extend her hand in formal greeting.

'Kahl,' he said, enclosing her hand in a fist that seemed to contain an electric charge.

Lucy snatched it free. 'Won't you sit down?' she said again, pointing to a chair at the far end of the table. She would feel a lot safer once he was seated.

'After you,' he said, drawing out a chair for her to sit on.

Lucy felt alert, and uneasy. All the other creditors had been up in arms, expressing their anger freely and paying no account to the fact that she was a woman. That was better. It was a language she understood. This man was too cool. He frightened her more than the others with their impassioned outbursts. Apart from confidence, he oozed sex appeal as the others had oozed sweat at the thought of losing money.

Dark flashing eyes smouldered like black coals in a face

with features too harsh to be conventionally handsome. He made her think of a warrior, a man of action—yet he had the type of tan she associated with the super-rich. Lucy frowned. So who was he? Apart from being one of the most incredible-looking individuals she had ever seen. Was he Turkish? Armenian? Spanish? She couldn't place the accent.

As the man folded his impressive frame into a chair across the table from her she judged him to be about thirty-five: dark-haired, dark-skinned, dark-eyed—and very expensively dressed. She had a keen eye for fashion, as well as for architecture. Jeans could be budget or designer, and his were the best, like the simple black top he was wearing.

As he levelled a stare on her face Lucy drew breath, forcing herself to hold his gaze. Without focusing on it, she was aware of his mouth. It was full and sensuous, with a cruel twist, matching the look in his eyes. After some heated discussion the rest of the creditors had believed her when she'd pledged to repay them. She sensed this man was different—harder, more cynical.

He shifted position, clearly uncomfortable on the narrow seat. Men just didn't come built like this—not in her world, anyhow. Even his casual clothes failed to conceal thighs made of iron, and shoulders wide enough to carry an ox.

Lucy dropped her gaze, conscious she was staring at him. And then her glance strayed to his hands. They were extremely powerful, but it didn't look as though he earned his living by them. As he reached back to fold his arms behind his head she saw his belly was flat— She had to stop this, Lucy told herself firmly. He was just one more aggrieved creditor. She owed it to him to spell out her position.

As if sensing she was ready, he tipped his head, inviting her to begin. Unlike the others, he had brought nothing with him, Lucy noticed, not even a pen to take notes. 'Well, Mr—'

'Kahl. Just call me Kahl,' he interrupted.

His dark eyes were tilted up at the corners, and his jet-black eyebrows swept up too. Like a Tartar's, she thought, wondering if he came from the steppes of Russia. Could he ride a horse as they did? A quiver ran through her as she pictured his powerful thighs wrapped around the sides of some wild stallion, or a woman—

'You have a proposition for me?'

Lucy felt herself reddening, as if he had read her mind. She rallied fast. 'I intend to pay everyone off fully—everything I owe you will be repaid,' she underlined when he appeared unmoved. Something in his stare was starting to get to her. 'Do you find this amusing?'

'Far from it,' he murmured, gesturing with his hand that she should continue.

Lucy bridled at the autocratic manner, but her sense of honour insisted she fulfil her obligations in full—even to this man. As he fingered his jaw she saw that it was shaded blue-black, even so early in the day. There was something so rampantly male about him that it made every feminine bone in her body rebel. It was a sensation she was determined to resist.

'So, you're with the architects?' she guessed, with nothing more to go on than a pair of strong, smooth hands.

'I heard that your impressive plans to renovate Westbury Hall had fallen through,' he replied.

She loved his voice. She couldn't help it. It was so foreign, so exotic— This was ridiculous! The look in his eyes was warning enough to keep her thoughts in check.

'I'm really sorry, but I've been forced to cancel all the contracts,' she said bluntly, judging the direct approach to be best. Dragging her briefcase towards her, Lucy fished inside. 'I should have yours here...'

'I doubt it.'

'I've prepared a schedule,' she said, frowning as she surfaced without any missing contract. 'You should look at this,' she said, holding out another document. 'It explains how I will pay everyone back for the services they have already provided. You can keep this copy.'

'I'll study it later,' he said, folding the pages neatly.

Lucy watched as he half stood to tuck the papers away in the back pocket of his jeans—and her gaze lingered. 'I'm sorry,' she said, with a helpless gesture when he turned and caught her staring. 'It's all I can offer you for now.'

He shrugged as he sat down again, and Lucy wondered if he was convinced by her little speech. 'That's it,' she said, when he showed no sign of moving. Did he expect something more? Lucy's heart began to thunder. 'Did you have to come far?' she said, in a voice that sounded higher than usual. When he didn't answer, she added, 'Have you been travelling long?'

'Half a day.'

'Half a day! I'm really sorry.' And she was—mortified. 'Can I offer you a drink or something?'

He shrugged. 'It's almost lunchtime.'

'Of course. Something more? We could go for a sandwich, perhaps?'

'The village pub is closed for renovation.'

Damn. She had forgotten about that. He *was* observant.

'I am hungry,' he admitted, easing back in his chair without breaking eye contact.

She was backed into a corner, Lucy realised. And now she was going to do something that was probably crazy. 'Why don't you come back to my place and I'll make you a sandwich?'

He stood at once, pushing his chair back, coming around the table to hold Lucy's chair for her.

She was definitely crazy—no doubt about it!

The man followed her into the low-ceilinged farmhouse kitchen, ducking to avoid the beams.

'The farmer must have been a lot shorter than you,' Lucy said, acting casually in spite of the frisson of awareness tracking down her back.

'So it seems.'

She felt him staring at her while she pretended to study the inside of the refrigerator as if she had no idea what was inside. 'Cheese? Pickle?'

'Whatever you have,' the exotic voice husked obligingly.

'Beer? Coffee?'

'Coffee would be great—or water.'

Yes. Water, of course. It was hot for early May.

The air seemed charged with unusual energy—but it was his energy, she realised, feeling the tiny hairs on the back of her neck stand to attention. 'You'd better sit down,' she suggested, turning around. 'Before you hit your head.'

'Thank you,' he said, moving to pull out the bench at the kitchen table.

And then it struck her forcibly. She didn't even know who he was! And here he was in her home. She had never done anything like this before—and was damn sure she would never risk anything like it again! But it wasn't every day her dreams hit the dust. Her emotions were in chaos, Lucy realised, quickly making excuses for herself.

'Aren't you going to have something to eat or drink?' he said.

'I'm not hungry,' she said, handing him a plate.

'If you won't eat, how can I?'

'Look. I don't mean to be rude—' Lucy wiped a hand across her forehead distractedly '—but exactly which company do you represent? You never said.'

'Why don't you sit down?' he suggested evenly.

'So?' Lucy prompted, perching on a stool well away from him at the breakfast bar. 'Which company did you say you worked for?'

'I didn't.' Leaning back comfortably in his seat, Kahl

looked at her. 'Do you invite many men you don't know into your home?'

'You haven't answered my question.'

'And you haven't answered mine,' he pointed out.

'Not many—I mean none.' Why was she making excuses to him? Lucy wondered, biting her lip.

'It's not safe.'

'I can assure you I don't make a habit of it. But—'

'But?' he cut in, spearing a glance at her.

'Today's different.'

He let that pass. 'You want to know which company I represent?' he said, pushing the plate away.

'Yes, I do.' He was right: this was dangerous. She didn't know a thing about him.

'I represent myself.'

'I see…'

'I doubt it.'

The atmosphere was electric and his confidence unsettling. It was as if he had planned this all along. 'I'll make coffee,' she offered, keen to put some distance between them.

'Don't bother—cold water will do.'

'It won't take a minute.'

He shrugged.

'Sugar? Milk?'

He said no to both.

She passed him the mug, and when their fingers touched Lucy gasped. It was as if a lightning bolt had shot up her arm.

'Did you scald yourself?' he asked with concern.

'No, I'm fine.'

'Sit?' he suggested, pulling out a chair for her.

She would sit—because she wasn't going to let him get to her—not in her own home, her own kitchen.

The kitchen table was narrow and his legs were long; they

almost touched her own. And then they did—shins, feet,
ankles—colliding, tangling briefly. When she tried to pull
away he hooked one of his legs around hers, and held her
fast.

She might have cried out softly as her heart leapt into her
throat; she certainly couldn't breathe. Lucy looked at him
wide-eyed, and for one insane moment she thought she
would fight him off, rain her fists down on his chest. But
that soon passed. The contact between them was so intimate,
so enticing. She knew she was lost.

'Still feeling safe?' he murmured.

Lucy dragged in an unsteady breath. 'Yes,' she said, lying
through her teeth as she held his gaze. She knew he could
overpower her in an instant. But he wouldn't. She was sure.
Not unless she wanted him to.

The silence was so intense that for a few seconds she
heard nothing but the sound of her own heart hammering in
her head. And then gradually she became aware of another
sound, rapid and noisy. When she realised it was the raised
pitch of her own breathing her cheeks flamed red.

The man's expression was inscrutable. He was waiting
for something—but for what? Was she supposed to make
the first move? Lucy wondered. He was temptation on a
plate. Ridiculously attractive, and with the X-factor that told
her he knew just how to please a woman. But it was the
look in his eyes that swung it for her. It held the promise
of forgetfulness, of oblivion. She could leave all the heart-
break and disappointment behind for a few hours. They
were consenting adults. He offered escape, and that was just
what she needed.

The chance to make love—have sex—with a complete
stranger was absurdly appealing. It was uncharted territory
for Lucy. She had always thought of sex as something between two people who knew each other well, who trusted
each other, felt safe.

But she was consumed by arousal. The decision was out of her hands; her senses were taking the lead. Every inch of her body was tuned to his frequency. The merest change in his eyes brought her to a fresh level of awareness, and just a tug at one corner of his mouth was enough to make her want to kiss away its harshness and feel him melt beneath her touch. It was appetite, pure and simple. Even words were redundant. They were communicating now on another, very basic level.

Taking hold of her wrist, Kahl brought her to a standing position in front of him. His touch shimmered through her and he dragged her close, so she felt the whole length of his body in intimate contact with her own. It was too late to regret the fact that she was only wearing a lightweight summer dress, with a scrap or two of lace beneath it—too late to regret the fact that where this man called Kahl was concerned she had no will-power at all.

He was more athletically built than any man she had known before. He was big, gloriously big, and his strength was deliciously contained—like a tightly wound spring. He smelt divine, he felt warm and hard, and as he teased her lips apart Lucy felt her legs grow weak. She could feel his heart beating strongly in his chest as it pressed against her breasts, and her own thundering against him. It was all new sensation, all heights of pleasure she hadn't known existed; it was like getting to know someone starting at the pinnacle and working back. He was as hard as marble, but far more fluid—

She gave a low cry of surprise when he swung her up without warning. Setting her on the table-edge, he lowered her back as he moved between her legs. Then, pushing up her summer skirt, he reached for her underwear, unbuttoning his fly at the same time…Lucy felt the silky pass of something warm and smooth, and then a second pass, before he gave her the tip, catching it just inside her until she cried

out and urged him on. When he took the prompt her breath
shot out of her lungs in surprise at the size of him, and he
waited until she was ready again.

Then the pleasure began. It was beyond anything Lucy
had known. He swept the plate and mug aside, and lifted
her legs to lock them around his waist. Now he could plunge
deeper still, until rhythmical cries of delight left her lips.
Each time he dealt her another long, firm stroke Lucy's
fingers bit mercilessly into buttocks of steel, until finally her
mind shut down completely and only sensation remained.

Drunk with ecstasy, at one point she called out, and he
stopped.

'No!' Lucy ground out desperately, realising he must
have taken her cry for reluctance. 'Don't stop. Don't ever
stop—' And she laughed softly, happily, gratefully when he
started to move again.

He brought her skilfully to the place she had wanted to
be, tipping her over the edge into oblivion, so that for a few
trance-like moments she found all the relief, all the escape
she needed. But the sensation was so intense she almost
passed out in his arms.

'Are you all right?'

He was breathing the words in her ear, Lucy realised, and
holding her full weight in his arms. She buried her head
self-consciously into his chest, so he couldn't see her face
or hear her struggling attempts to catch her breath. Now it
was over, and the exquisite tremors were subsiding, she really couldn't believe what they had just done.

'I said, are you all right?' he said again, softly. And,
cupping her chin with one hand, he brought her head up so
she had no alternative but to look him straight in the eyes.

'I'm fine,' Lucy said, swallowing hard. But she felt naked, as if his eyes had the power to strip her defences away.
And his eyes were not black, but darkest sienna, she saw,

with flecks of molten copper round his pupil—incredible, astonishing.

'Don't look away,' he insisted, bringing her round to face him again. 'Bed?' he suggested, one eyebrow arching slightly. 'You do have one?' he murmured, when Lucy remained silent.

'Yes, of course,' she said, straightening her clothes self-consciously. 'You must be tired.'

'Far from it,' Kahl assured her, one corner of his mouth tugging up in the beginnings of a smile. 'I'm only just getting started.'

Linking his arms around her waist, he pulled her close again, nuzzling his crotch into the swell of her hips.

'Well, in that case…' Lucy felt hunger flare inside her. She hadn't had enough of him, not nearly enough.

Taking him by the hand, she moved towards the hallway. But playing the vamp didn't come naturally to her, and she hesitated by the door.

'Just say if you want me to leave,' Kahl murmured, drawing her into his arms, 'and I'll go.'

'No,' Lucy said quickly, softly. 'I don't want that.'

'Then, if you're sure…' he said, slamming into her senses with one of his slow-burning smiles.

'I'm sure,' she said, raising her face for his kiss.

There was a moment of hazy contentment on waking, then full-blown horror and distress. She was alone! Of course she was alone, Lucy told herself, staring round the bedroom. What the hell had she expected? A one-night stand—admittedly the most memorable one-night stand in history—did not a relationship make.

Dragging up the bedclothes to cover herself, she buried her head in the pillow, conscious that every inch of her was still throbbing from the attentions of a most accomplished lover. There would never be anyone like Kahl in her life again, that much was sure. No one could be that unselfish in the delivery of pleasure, no one so tender when they held her in their arms. And now he was gone.

Lucy swallowed hard, tears stinging the back of her throat, knowing she only had herself to blame. No one had forced her to sleep with him. She had gone into it with her eyes wide open, giving herself yet one more disaster to recover from.

Getting out of bed, Lucy headed for the bathroom. A long, hot shower was a start—not much of a start, but the rest of her life would not go away.

And then she saw the flowers sitting on her dressing table in a glass tumbler. He must have cut them fresh from her garden, she realised, before he left: early roses, her favourite Lochinvar, blush-pink, fat, and lightly fragranced.

Touching the cool, dew-damp petals with her fingertips, she felt a shiver of apprehension run down her spine.

CHAPTER TWO

RAGS to riches? Not exactly, Lucy thought as she lolled back in the plush leather seat. But she was getting there. Since winning the design competition her life had certainly undergone a meteoric change. She had repaid her creditors, and was slowly building up her business again.

It was good to know that hard work and determination paid off occasionally, she thought, glancing round at her fellow travellers. Several passengers in the first-class cabin smiled back and raised their glasses. Buoyed up by complimentary champagne, Lucy radiated happiness and optimism.

Normally she was quite frightened of flying, and travelled by other means wherever she could. But the chance to fly first class with Air Abadan had been irresistible, and she hadn't been allowed to feel one flutter of unease since the smiling attendant had welcomed her on board.

It hardly seemed possible that seat belts were already being checked for landing. And, having left England in icy February, neither could she believe the announcement that it was a balmy twenty-five degrees in the desert kingdom of Abadan.

Abadan. Just the name of the country was enough to spark Lucy's imagination. Which was just as well, since the first prize in the competition was a lucrative contract to carry out the refurbishment of a receiving room at the Golden Palace. She had put everything she had into her entry, knowing it was a once-in-a-lifetime opportunity. The brief had been demanding, as quite a bit of restoration was needed before superficial decorative work could begin. Fortunately, sourcing the type of craftsmen who could restore the golden filigree that gave the Golden Palace its name was just the type of challenge she liked.

Winning was fantastic, but preparing the project had given her a second chance, and that was even more important. Even the lingering anger she had still felt over the bank letting her down had faded away as she'd been drawn deeper into her work. Interestingly enough, the sale of Westbury Hall had realised far more than she had anticipated, allowing her to clear her debts and make some provision for the future. But as far as business was concerned she was determined to concentrate on what she knew best, and that was interior design.

At the awards ceremony, at a swanky London hotel, Lucy remembered the Abadanese ambassador announcing that she had won because she'd gone the extra mile for his client. According to him, she had uncovered facts that even the ruling family was not aware of. It had made her smile at the time, and she smiled now, draining her glass.

The 'ruling family' was the one element she had found impossible to research in any detail. The Sheikh and his son remained shadowy figures. For security reasons, she guessed. Sensible, really. She didn't expect to meet up with them. And she wasn't unduly concerned. The design brief she had been given was quite specific, and she had already embellished it with her own suggestions. Passing ideas to and fro by e-mail was an easy matter. And everything she had submitted so far had been met with a positive response. She didn't anticipate any difficulties.

'Which is just as well, my darling,' she crooned, double-checking the safety harness on the travel cot by her side as the plane came in to land, 'since you're going to be celebrating your first birthday in Abadan.'

*　*　*

It wasn't every day she got to stay in a palace, Lucy thought, reining in her excitement as she tried to take everything in amid the overload of visual information. She had hardly believed it when the Sheikh's representative, a smartly dressed middle-aged woman, had explained almost apologetically that she was being housed in one of the older parts of the palace.

The palace! Lucy had been expecting to stay in a nearby hotel. But the palace accommodation deemed suitable for her had a nursery attached...

'Oh, yes, everything is more than satisfactory. Thank you,' Lucy said, hardly able to believe where she was. And if this was shabby, as the woman seemed to imply, she couldn't wait to see smart!

The older woman looked relieved. 'And Leila will take care of your son,' she said, turning to introduce a young girl who was standing in the background.

Lucy felt instantly reassured. Leila wore the casual uniform of a Barton nanny. The chinos and white polo shirt with the distinctive 'B' embroidered on the breast pocket marked her out as a top professional in her field. Originally Lucy had planned to leave Edward at home with his grandmother, but an unseasonal bout of influenza had put paid to that idea. The officials she had been speaking to at the palace had quickly reassured her. Edward would be well looked after in Abadan, they said. 'What's the problem? Bring him with you.'

The prospect of missing her child's first birthday had been terrible, but miraculously fate had conspired to keep them together. So now she could enjoy Edward's birthday and begin to secure his future, with the money she expected to earn from the contract.

'What do you think of Abadan so far?' Edward's newly appointed nanny asked, reclaiming her attention.

'Fantastic,' Lucy admitted. 'The scenery on the drive from the airport to the palace was amazing—rolling sand dunes stretching away to the horizon, and then,' she said, her face animated as she remembered, 'when the sun dropped lower, there were camels marching in procession along the hilltops, inky-black silhouettes against a dazzling vermilion sky.'

'You do like it.' Leila laughed. 'Can I take him?' She smiled at Edward.

Lucy hesitated only a moment, then, seeing Edward's reaction, she said, 'Of course. It looks like you've made a friend of him already, Leila.'

Lucy relaxed. If Edward was happy she knew everything would go smoothly. It was beginning to look as if his first birthday was going to be every bit as memorable as she had always hoped it would be.

Padding barefoot around her spacious quarters in her pyjamas with Edward soon after dawn, Lucy felt happier than she could remember for a long time. And, despite a restless night, she was on good form, too, she realised, hugging her wriggling bundle a little closer.

Edward constantly exclaimed and pointed as they explored the opulent interior together. Even the incredible height of the ceilings inside their suite of rooms was a revelation to him, and he was growing increasingly hard to carry as he leaned back in Lucy's arms to marvel at them.

Blowing her hair out of her face, Lucy laughed out loud with sheer happiness. She felt a growing conviction that this trip to Abadan marked a new start in life for both of them. The prestige that came with winning the competition meant her professional future was more assured, which in turn meant things would be better for Edward. And everything she did was for him.

Her life was one big balancing act, but—touch wood—it was going well, and she wouldn't have it any other way. She knew she mustn't get complacent. She couldn't risk anything going wrong later that morning in her first meeting. But there was little chance of that. She had been up half the night, pacing the room, as she went over everything in her mind.

And she wasn't the only early riser, Lucy remembered, dropping a kiss on the top of Edward's head. At one point something had drawn her to a window overlooking the interior courtyard. But by the time she'd leaned out there had been just a shadow disappearing through one of the arched doors facing her apartment.

She glanced out of the window at the same archway now, remembering that shortly afterwards the whole palace had sprung to life—temperatures later in the day would be less conducive to activity, she supposed. Then, thinking of the shadow again, she shivered involuntarily.

Edward's baby prattle stopped immediately, and he turned his face up to look at her.

'It's all right, my darling,' Lucy crooned, turning his attention to a pair of vases taller than she was, to make him laugh again.

The shadow, Lucy reassured herself, had doubtless been one of the servants who had left his bed ahead of the rest...*his*? His bed? She thought about it for a moment. The shadow had been long, and the impression she'd gained when she caught a glimpse of it had been of a man—a large man—one of the palace guards, perhaps?

'Miss Benson?'

Lucy turned, smiling, as Leila hurried towards her across the vast marble-tiled floor. It took a few words of reassurance before Leila would be convinced she wasn't late, and that Edward's early start to the day was due entirely to Lucy's excitement.

It was fun arranging Edward's day together. When her meeting with the palace officials was over, Lucy was determined they should do something about a birthday tea for him the next day. But as they discussed the particulars she became increasingly conscious of time slipping away—and she wasn't even showered or dressed yet.

'Don't worry,' Leila said, 'I'll start making enquiries while you are in your meeting—' She stopped talking as Edward claimed their attention.

'He wants to go to the window for some fresh air,' Lucy guessed. 'Try and get him outside to play while it's cool, if you can. He's got far too much energy to be cooped up in here all day.'

'I will,' Leila promised.

Lucy was halfway across the room when Leila called her back.

'Come and see this,' she insisted, beckoning to Lucy. 'Quickly.'

'What is it?' Lucy said, hurrying to join Leila and Edward by the open window. She was struck by Edward's unusual stillness as he stared down from his grandstand position in Leila's arms.

Following Edward's lead, Lucy gazed down into the courtyard. A group of men in flowing robes were striding across it at speed. She felt a thrill of excitement. There was something so majestic in their carriage, so romantic. It really brought home to her the fact that she was a guest in a great desert kingdom. The men looked nothing short of magnificent, with their white *gutrahs* held in place by *agals* of black and gold, and the man spearheading the group was particularly striking. He was clearly the leader in every respect. She smiled to see a shorter man scurrying along at his elbow, trying to keep up as he mouthed notes into a small black Dictaphone.

'That's Prince Kahlil ben Saeed Al-Sharif—the ruling Sheikh's son,' Leila explained, seeing Lucy's interest. 'He practically rules Abadan now. His father is retiring more and more from public life. They say Sheikh Kahlil will take over full responsibility for the country very soon.'

'What else do they say?' Lucy murmured as the men disappeared through an archway.

'They say Abadan is going to be catapulted into the twenty-first century, thanks to Sheikh Kahlil,' Leila confided. 'He's already hugely successful in the international business world. And he's gorgeous—'

'I'd better get ready for my meeting,' Lucy cut in diplomatically. She had to remain professional. However tempting it might be, she knew she couldn't afford to be drawn into palace gossip.

CHAPTER THREE

COOLLY yet smartly dressed, in a long-sleeved tunic and wide-legged pants in cream linen, Lucy knew she was as ready for the meeting as she would ever be. And she had no excuse to get flustered; she didn't even have to carry her own design portfolio. She was being spoiled, she realised as the young man in Western dress who had come to escort her to the meeting lifted it out of her hands. Better not get used to this, she mused wryly, following him down an echoing corridor.

Lucy's heart was thundering as her companion opened the door of the vaulted council chamber. Silence fell as she entered, then a wave of sound rolled over her as everyone rose from their seats at once. Head held high, she walked towards a lozenge-shaped table she judged to be about thirty feet in length, around which men in the flowing robes of Arabia were standing—*waiting for her*...

Lucy's throat dried. Her earlier optimism appeared premature. Her confidence was evaporating now she was faced with the reality of the scale, opulence, and importance that was attached to the project. It was an awesome responsibility.

Fortunately, before doubt really set in, the young man accompanying her placed her portfolio on the table and pulled out a chair for her. Pinning what she hoped was a professional expression to her face, she sat down. At this signal everyone else sat too. Then an older man to her left leaned across.

'His Majesty apologises,' he murmured. 'He will be a little late. But if you would care to give a brief outline to his council in the meantime, he will join the meeting as soon as he can.'

Lucy dipped her head in polite acknowledgement of this news.

She would have preferred to get the meet-and-greet part of things over with right away. But now she had to begin, knowing that at any moment the ruler of Abadan or his son might interrupt. It couldn't be helped. She would just have to get on with it regardless.

She had just completed her formal introduction to the presentation when the double doors suddenly parted with some ceremony. Unaccountably, she started to shake with nerves. All the men seated at the table with her rose at once, and turned in the direction of the entrance. This was ridiculous, Lucy told herself, drawing a few deep, steadying breaths. She hadn't felt anything quite like it since—

'His Majesty.'

Lucy remained standing sideways on to the door as an unseen courtier announced the Sheikh's arrival in English. Out of consideration for her, no doubt, she presumed. And then curiosity got the better of her, and she turned.

The striking individual who strode into the room supported by a phalanx of following attendants was too young to be the ruling Sheikh. This must be his son, Lucy guessed, and, remembering the figure in the courtyard, she felt her heart begin to race. He had such incredible presence. She felt as if she was looking at someone on a screen, from a distance. It was like looking at Hollywood's best ever stab at an Arabian prince—except that the man coming towards her was the real thing, and she knew instinctively that there was absolutely nothing contrived about him.

The sun streaming in from glass panels above the entrance doors was preventing her from seeing him properly. But she didn't need to see the man clearly to sense the aura of power he carried with him. And it was a forbidding power. He would have to be a hard man, Lucy reminded herself. Sheikh Kahlil of Abadan was a prince of the desert, a warrior through and through. He would have to be the type of individual to inspire confidence and fear in equal measure to win the respect of his people.

He covered the distance between them in a few strides, black robes billowing around him as he walked. The plain black *gutrah* on his head, captured by a gold *agal*, masked what little of his face the blinding sunlight allowed her to see.

'Miss Benson,' he murmured coolly, extending his hand Western-style in greeting.

He was much taller than she had imagined. Standing so close, he eclipsed the rest of the room. They might have been alone. Automatically Lucy grasped his hand.

As they touched, a tremor struck that jolted through every inch of her. She drew a fast breath as it pulsed through every fibre, every muscle, every nerve-ending—

'Majesty,' she managed to murmur, pulling her hand away as if he had burned her. She kept her head lowered, more to avoid the harsh, assessing stare than as a gesture of respect.

'Gentlemen,' she heard him say politely, 'please be seated. Don't let me throw you off stride—please continue,' he added to Lucy with an elegant gesture.

But there was something extra in his voice now, undetectable to those around them, but menacingly apparent to Lucy. For a moment she couldn't speak. A tornado had been let loose inside her. Her mind was in freefall, her heartbeat suspended. She gasped involuntarily, noisily, once, then became aware of the interest she was generating around the table, and swiftly gathered her wits.

'Yes, yes, of course,' she said hastily.

'Water for Miss Benson,' Sheikh Kahlil said, leaning back ever so slightly in his seat to direct the servants.

It couldn't possibly be, Lucy told herself desperately. She gratefully took the glass of water someone handed to her. Could the Kahl she knew have an identical twin. A *doppelgänger* in Abadan he knew nothing about? She took a few sips, and then made herself look up and smile reassuringly round the table. She had heard it said that everyone had a double somewhere in the world, and had always thought it nonsense. But perhaps, just this once, it was true?

'Yes, thank you. I'm ready to continue now.' Lucy was amazed by the steadiness of her voice. Under the circumstances it was nothing short of a miracle! But her thoughts swung wildly back and forth like a pendulum. Was Sheikh Kahlil Kahl? In her heart, Lucy already knew the answer. The man sitting just inches away from her, calmly arranging the folds of his robe, was Edward's father! And he didn't even know he had a son.

Suddenly Lucy was overwhelmed by fear. What might a man as powerful as Sheikh Kahlil do when he discovered he had a son? She had brought Edward into danger—

'Miss Benson? Would you care to continue?'

The Sheikh's tone was neutral, but it unnerved her. He had recognised her too, she was certain of it. How much time would she have before someone told him she was not alone…that she had her baby son with her?

Feeling his scrutiny, Lucy refocused quickly. 'Yes, of course. Forgive me, gentlemen…the heat…'

The heat! Air-conditioning in the palace didn't allow for a moment's discomfort. She would have to do better than that. But Lucy felt as if she was tumbling down a deep black hole. Her heart was thundering out of control, and her mind was paralysed with anxiety. Somehow she had to continue, and get through this—for Edward's sake, if not for her own. Once the meeting was over and she was in the privacy of her own room she would have space to think—to work out how she could get away from Abadan with Edward.

Now she knew the true identity of the man she thought of as Kahl, she would seek legal advice. Of course Edward should know who his father was. And she would tell him when the time was right... Lucy glanced around as if seeing everything again for the first time. How could she ever compete with this? How could she deny her son such a heritage? The thought chilled her, but she was careful not to arouse suspicion, and focused all her attention on the meeting.

How she got through the rest of the morning, Lucy had no idea. On the few occasions that Kahlil addressed her directly he confined his questions to the project. But his keenness of mind alarmed her. She realised she hadn't taken his intellect into account at their first meeting—she had been too distracted by his other qualities. But now she saw that no detail was too small to escape his attention, and as he probed the minutiae of her plans her fears began to grow.

Nothing *ever* slipped through his guard, Kahlil raged inwardly. But he had entrusted the competition and all it entailed to one of his advisors. This meeting had been arranged so that he could congratulate the winner, and meet them in person, and it signalled his first real involvement in a project intended to bring Abadan to the notice of the world. He was determined that his heirs would one day inherit a country at the forefront of exclusive holiday destinations, and the PR resulting from the design competition, together with the opening of the Golden Palace to the public, was crucial to that plan.

And then this had come about. *How?* Kahlil wondered grimly. He had asked for The Best, and they had brought him Lucy Benson! But she could hardly have been expected to make the connection on paper, he supposed, snapping a suspicious glance at Lucy. Twenty-one months ago he had told her his name was Kahl, nothing more.

They had enjoyed each other. That should have been an

end of it. He wasn't in the habit of inviting trouble into his life.

The competition had been set up to maximise publicity and to encourage entries from a broad range of entrants—not just the usual celebrity designers. His aim had been to discover new talent. Well, that had certainly worked, Kahlil reflected grimly. Lucy Benson had hit the ground running, winning this prestigious design contract less than a couple of years after setting up again in business, by his reckoning.

The competition had been supposed to find a new face for him to launch, with photographs of the winner flashed around the world, raising the profile of Abadan at the same time. But he had been thinking of attracting the best designers when he'd set it up, not women with questionable morals—though, as that went, Lucy Benson was still the best, Kahlil conceded, feeling his senses flare. Within minutes of their first meeting he had taken her on her kitchen table. There had been something so potent between them even he hadn't been able to resist the temptation. She had made him lose control to the point where he'd mated with her like a ravening beast, with no thought for the consequences! But it would never happen again.

He had nothing to reproach himself for, Kahlil reflected, turning the events of almost two years ago over in his mind. They had both been consenting adults. And he had made the break nice and clean, leaving before she woke—no regrets, no recriminations—better for both of them that way.

Kahlil's anger at finding himself in such an embarrassing position simmered dangerously close to the surface as he chaired the meeting. In spite of his best endeavours, his underlying thoughts remained stubbornly fixed on Lucy Benson. Was it coincidence or contrivance that had brought her to Abadan? He had been present when her dreams were shattered. Every detail of that day had to be etched on her mind. Had she somehow managed to discover his true identity after their brief and passionate encounter? It hardly seemed likely, but history proved how cunning women could be when a kingdom and a fortune were at stake. He would have to be on his guard, and wait to see what new surprises she might spring on him. Maybe she was innocent, maybe not; only time would tell.

Lucy had never been more relieved to wind up a meeting. It had gone well. No one, not even Kahlil, could fault the meticulous way in which she had prepared her submission for approval. As the room emptied, she kept her head down and concentrated on collecting up all her drawings and samples. Finally only Kahlil and the young man who had escorted her to the meeting remained.

'You may go,' Kahlil said, turning to his young aide. 'I will assist Miss Benson.'

Lucy's swift intake of breath sounded loud in the vaulted chamber, but by the time she lifted her head to protest the young aide was a distant figure, moving swiftly towards the door.

'That's all right, I can manage,' she said calmly, straightening up to confront Kahlil. Standing in silence just a few feet away from her, he was a menacing sight.

'I wish to speak to you,' he said.

He kept his voice low, but it was authoritarian and chilling. There was no 'wish' about it, Lucy thought immediately. Here in Abadan Kahlil's wish was a command. And she dared not challenge him just yet. 'Of course,' she said quietly.

'We will take lunch together—'

He made it sound about as appealing as sitting down to eat with a wounded tiger.

'—in the city,' he informed her.

Lucy felt some relief. Anywhere away from the palace, away from Edward, would do. 'OK,' she agreed, meeting

Kahlil's gaze. But her heart was banging in her chest, and her mind was a whirlwind of thoughts, all clashing together so that she couldn't make sense of anything other than the need to keep Kahlil away from Edward until she could get them both safely out of Abadan.

Kahlil's dark gaze never left her face for an instant, almost as if he could probe her guilty thoughts. But Lucy reckoned if she could confine their discussion to work over lunch she might just get away with it and buy some time. The Golden Palace was so vast it was unlikely their paths would ever cross again.

No wonder he'd left before she woke on that occasion, Lucy reflected angrily. As far as Sheikh Kahlil was concerned she'd provided a few hours' distraction. He was the heir to a kingdom. Pleasurable time spent in bed with a woman was hardly a world-shattering event for him. It was certainly not a good enough reason for him to stay and play happy families with her the next day, Lucy reflected cynically, angry that her body insisted on behaving as if Kahlil was the answer to her dreams—nightmare, more like, she warned herself, pinning a cool, professional smile back on her face.

'I'll just take my things back to my room and then I'll meet you—'

'Leave everything here. It will all be collected and delivered to your rooms—I trust everything is to your satisfaction?' he said.

'Extremely pleasant,' Lucy said. The last thing she wanted was for him to decide to check up on her accommodation for himself. 'Shouldn't I get changed for lunch?' she asked, looking for an excuse to return to Edward. She longed for the sanctuary of the nursery. Dining with the devil was not her recreation of choice.

'You are perfect as you are.'

Lucy's heart sank. She couldn't risk raising Kahlil's suspicions. She had no option but to go with him.

The words had rushed out before he could stop himself, Kahlil thought impatiently. But it was true, unfortunately; as a women and a bedmate Lucy Benson *was* perfect.

Maybe this surprise reunion wasn't so annoying after all. His lips began to curve in sardonic appreciation of the situation. The photographs that had been taken during the meeting, of him presenting a prestigious design prize to exciting new talent Miss Lucy Benson, would be flashed around the world—but no one would guess at their earlier involvement. Life moved in mysterious circles—but she was here; he might as well make use of her.

CHAPTER FOUR

SUSPENDED two hundred metres above the Gulf of Abadan, the restaurant Kahlil had chosen for lunch was exceptional in every way: opulent, hushed, clearly very expensive, and full of what Lucy immediately classed as 'beautiful people'.

The clientele certainly wasn't composed of run-of-the-mill couples, she noticed, looking around, and she wondered if that explained why Kahlil had chosen here, rather than the palace, for their meeting. Separate booths, high-backed, with velvet padded seats in crimson, allowed a degree of privacy that for some reason Lucy found alarming. Their lunchtime companions were men in flowing robes accompanied by young and beautiful companions wearing the latest fashions and fabulous jewellery.

'What kind of place is this?' she said. 'I thought we were having a working lunch.'

'Discreet,' Kahlil said crisply. The *maître d'* escorted him straight towards one of the best tables, overlooking the Gulf.

A place to take your mistress! The thought leapt into Lucy's head like an unwelcome thorn. This wasn't a business meeting, it was a negotiation, she thought angrily. Kahlil remembered everything about their first encounter, and wanted to cut a deal before they returned to the palace.

There was considerable interest as they crossed the room together, with Kahlil well ahead of her, and Lucy's face flamed red as she realised what he was subjecting her to. Tilting her chin a little higher, she smiled faintly and pinned a look of confidence to her face. The first chance she got she was out of here! She would never allow Edward to see his mother humiliated in such a way.

With a polite word of thanks, Lucy accepted the seat the *maître d'* drew out for her. Then she noticed the bodyguards stationed at all the exits: discreet men in Western dress with jackets designed to conceal a holster. A shiver ran down her spine, reminding her that her escape would amount to treason. Whisking the son of the heir to the throne of Abadan out of the country without his father's knowledge or approval would be madness—but what alternative did she have? Losing her son just wasn't an option.

Sheikh Kahlil ben Saeed Al-Sharif was Edward's father! Lucy's stomach clenched with apprehension as she stole a look at the man seated across the table from her.

Kahlil was a forbidding figure in his flowing black Arab garb. He was unmistakably a prince, a warrior prince—she amended, seeing the discreet and reverent glances he was attracting. Everyone deferred to him. It was as if the pitch of the voices around them had been turned down a couple of notches. And even the waiters seemed to be handling the china and glass carefully so that they made less clatter.

Lucy shook her head faintly as the *maître d'* approached to discuss the menu with him. It hardly seemed possible that Sheikh Kahlil—for suddenly she could think of him no other way than as a sheikh—was the same casually dressed man she had given herself to so eagerly, hoping for oblivion, for a few hours of relief... She must have been mad! She was mad, Lucy thought anxiously. Did she really think she was going to be able to hide the fact that she had a baby from him? Her thoughts travelled back to the nursery, to Edward. Maybe it would be safer for him if she just folded and gave in.

Lucy glanced at some of the other young women in the room. Most were smiling happily at their wealthy and powerful companions, and quite a few were laughing—but this wasn't the life for her. Lucy knew that for a fact. She was who she was, and had to take the consequences. She could only hope that one day Edward would understand.

Lucy took little part in ordering the food. On every point where it was possible to compromise she intended to do so. If it pleased Sheikh Kahlil to order for her, so be it. But she would not compromise her honour, her career, or Edward's happiness—in reverse order, Lucy determined, levelling a steady stare on his face.

'So, Lucy,' he began easily, 'this is a pleasant surprise.'

Not, Lucy thought, reading the sub-text behind his hard gaze.

'It's been a long time. Almost two years; a lot must have happened in that time.'

She had been dreading this moment, the moment when he finally acknowledged their first encounter. But now it had come, and she had survived it. She relaxed a little, and gave a fairly comprehensive run-down of her professional life, but nothing more. She would not succumb, at least outwardly, to the glint of knowledge in his dark eyes that told her Sheikh Kahlil was remembering every moment of their first X-rated encounter, and was now prompting her to do the same.

As if she could forget, Lucy thought, toying with the food, glad that the constant supply of new dishes filled any awkward gaps in their conversation.

'Won't you have some pudding, or coffee?' he said, when at last the meal was over.

'No, thank you,' Lucy said, folding her napkin. She had exhausted every topic of conversation in the safety zone. All she wanted now was to return to the palace—to Edward—and make plans to get home safely with him before Sheikh Kahlil learned the truth about her son and tried to stop her.

'I'll take you back.'

He stood, and instantly an entourage seemed to materialise from nowhere and surrounded them. As he waved them away, Lucy's heart thundered a warning. His suggestion was far too intimate for comfort. They had arrived at the restaurant in a chauffeur-driven limousine. What did he have in mind now?

He was devastatingly attractive, Lucy conceded as she got up from the table. It would be the easiest thing in the world to fall into bed with him. Sheikh Kahlil terrified her and attracted her in equal measure, and that was a potent mix. Just the thought of being the one woman who could tame him, who could melt his icy heart, would have been an irresistible challenge to anyone. But that was a foolish daydream, and, however many notches he had on his Arabian bedpost, she had no intention of adding one more.

'Thank you. I'll get straight to work when we get back,' she lied, thinking of Edward.

Did Lucy Benson really imagine she was fooling him? Kahlil mused as he led the way out of the restaurant. Her prim manner was something new, admittedly, but he would soon strip that away.

At the door, one of his bodyguards handed him the keys to another car: something black, and very fast, and just big enough for two. He was in a hurry to get back to the palace now. He had waited long enough. Lucy Benson had had the audacity to avoid his questions, and he wanted to know why. What had she been up to over the past months? How many lovers had she enjoyed in that time?

Before quitting the restaurant Kahlil shut his eyes for a moment to compose himself. The fact that he still wanted Lucy was an inconvenience, but not one he intended to tolerate for very much longer. She had aroused his suspicions. There was something different about her, something he couldn't quite pin down. She was far more composed, and more confident than he remembered. She must have found contentment. *With a man?* The stab of jealousy took him by surprise as he swept through the door ahead of her. He couldn't remember such a thing happening before.

Having taken a few steps, Kahlil realised suddenly that he was alone. Lucy was still standing on the other side of the door. Impatiently he went back, meaning to chivvy her along, but the moment he reached her she sailed past—even finding time to grant *him* a gracious nod on the way!

However attractive Kahlil ben Saeed Al-Sharif might be, she would never allow him to humiliate her, Lucy thought, determined to start as she meant to go on.

She sat in silence as he gunned the engine of his custom-built Maserati into life, and guessed that here, in his own country, Kahlil bowed to nothing and no one. But as far as Lucy was concerned the common courtesies of life still applied. She *was* frightened—for herself, and for Edward most of all—but that was no reason to cave in and allow Kahlil to walk roughshod over her. Any sign of weakness would only harm them both in the long run. She would have to play a waiting game—act cautiously until an opportunity to escape presented itself.

It had been a huge shock to discover the father of her son in Abadan, and an even greater shock to realise the position he held. But she had to get over it fast. There was no time to dwell on the odds stacked against her. She had to look for the positives... But Sheikh Kahlil was not your run-of-the-mill adversary. He was the supreme challenge: the one man in the world she couldn't have; the one man in the world any woman in her right mind would want. And she did. Stealing a glance at him, Lucy found herself shuddering with something she longed to be cold, or apprehension—anything but desire.

The sexual tension between them was incredible, Kahlil reflected, and all the more so because they were confined in the body of the low-slung sports car. The air between them positively crackled with energy—energy that would have to find expression somehow. Maybe he would have pudding brought to his apartment, a platter of sweet pancakes, perhaps, and then he would feed her. And when she was accustomed once more to accepting pleasure at his hands he would take her to bed. Even the most fractious of his racehorses had learned to trust him, and Lucy Benson would do the same.

There was much similarity between the woman sitting next to him and the thoroughbreds in his stable. Both were proud, and edgy, and both could be soothed and persuaded to give of their best if sufficient patience was employed. And Lucy Benson was lucky; even after her insolence at the restaurant, he would grant her the rest of the day—by which time, like the best of his Arabian steeds, she would be begging him for a good workout.

When they arrived back at the palace, a member of Kahlil's council was waiting for him at the grand entrance.

'We will meet later,' Kahlil said to Lucy after a few hushed words with the man, 'to finish our meal and to talk further.'

Lucy's heart thumped ominously. Her fate wasn't settled, it was simply put on hold. But at least it gave her chance to go to Edward. 'When shall I see you?' she said, wanting to be prepared, and well away from Edward.

'In one hour,' Kahlil informed her. 'Someone will escort you to my rooms, and my chef will prepare some delicious dessert for us.'

It was a relief to know he wouldn't come to collect her, but it was also like sand running too fast through an hourglass, Lucy thought, managing a smile. Anyone might tell Kahlil she had brought a child with her. She could only trust he had more important things on his mind than palace gossip. But time was running out.

Edward was asleep when she returned to the nursery. 'No,

let him sleep,' she said to Leila. 'It can't do him any harm. He will still be suffering from jet lag, I expect.'

'We want him bright and breezy for his birthday tomorrow,' Leila agreed, looking down fondly at Edward's sleeping form.

'Yes,' Lucy agreed, feeling her throat tighten. 'But I'd better get back now—to finish my meeting with the Sheikh.'

'Don't worry about us,' Leila said, looking with concern at Lucy's tense face. 'We'll be fine. Just you relax—enjoy your meeting.'

If only, Lucy thought as she hurried out of the room.

It was easy to understand how she had succumbed so easily to Kahlil, Lucy realised as she watched him fork up the last delicious scraps of pancake for her. And perhaps he wasn't as bad as she thought. The harsh contours of his face seemed so much softer in the candlelight.

Even though it was still only late afternoon, they might have been in a luxurious pavilion at twilight, for he had instructed the servants to draw the silk blinds, and light dozens of candles for them. It was a fairytale setting.

The ceiling was tented with exquisite fabric in a rich ruby-red, and the windows behind the delicately printed blinds were tinted, to protect the room's occupants from the harsh midday sun. Kahlil had chosen well. If some form of compact was possible between them, this was the perfect setting. And sooner or later he would have to know about Edward. She wanted to trust him. It would be wonderful if she could.

She risked a small smile as she leaned across to take a second mouthful of the warm pudding from his fork. It was dripping with orange-flavoured sauce. She laughed, embarrassed, reaching for her napkin, but he was too quick for her.

'It's running down your chin,' he pointed out softly.

'I'm sorry.'

'Don't be.'

Before Lucy knew what he was doing, Kahlil had captured the drop of sauce at the corner of her mouth with his fingertip. 'It was careless of me to feed you that last mouthful so clumsily. I'm surprised you don't reprimand me.'

As their gazes locked, Lucy felt a bolt of sensation rip through her at the thought of chastising Sheikh Kahlil of Abadan. He had tapped unerringly into one of her most seductive fantasies.

'It is my responsibility,' he continued softly, 'to make sure that when I feed you everything goes in your mouth...'

Lucy swallowed hard as he put his now sauce-coated fingertip into his mouth and sucked it clean.

'Coffee?' he murmured, holding her stare.

There was no mistaking the real question in his eyes—and it had no connection with coffee. Lucy sucked in a few steadying breaths, but it did no good. Her heart was beating out of control. *He still wanted her.* He couldn't have made it more obvious. They could simply pick up where they had left off...

Madness! She couldn't think of it! She mustn't think of it, Lucy thought, angry with herself as she remembered that her first concern was to get Edward safely away from Abadan. Only then could she seek professional advice regarding his legal position.

'Coffee,' she said firmly.

'Why are you so shy now?' Kahlil asked, turning back to her after giving his instructions to the servants and then dismissing them. 'Isn't it a little late for modesty? Or is there someone else in your life?'

'There's no one,' Lucy confessed.

'No one?' Kahlil repeated, raising one ebony brow in wry amusement. 'Then what is the matter, Lucy? Why are you so reluctant to tell me anything about your private life?'

Lucy's knuckles went white as her hands balled into fists at her side. 'I have to get back—'

'Do you want to?'

Her hesitation was a beat too long. As Kahlil reached for her hand Lucy felt herself grow weak—not at the strength of him, as his power closed around her, but at the tantalising delicacy of his touch. He drew her onward by silken threads of desire, slowly, gently, like one of his most diffident mares. And as his hold on her increased, she melted. He felt so strong, so warm, and so uncannily familiar. It was as if they had never been apart, she realised, breathing faster. And then they were on their feet, facing each other, and she was longing for him to kiss her, for him to take her in his arms so that once again she could forget—

Forget! She could forget nothing, Lucy realised, coming to with a jolt. This wasn't a matter of her pride, or even her hopes and dreams—this was Edward's future, his security, his happiness. He belonged with her. She couldn't, wouldn't, do anything, *anything* to put that at risk. 'I have to go.'

Kahlil reached out and teased a few strands of her hair.

'I mean it, Kahlil,' she said, closing her eyes against the look in his eyes and the sensuous curl of his mouth.

'I won't stop you,' he said, knowing she wanted to stay. And he wanted her to stay. But he sensed that she was wound up like a spring. Another question without an answer, he reflected, staring keenly down at her.

Did he care? Kahlil almost laughed out loud. The hard man of Abadan discovering he had a heart? This was dangerous territory where a woman was concerned, and not a place he cared to visit. 'You are free to go,' he said coolly, standing back from her.

Lucy guessed that anything other than a direct command from Kahlil could never have resulted in someone leaving his presence so abruptly. She had to be cautious. 'I'm sure you have things to do too,' she said pleasantly.

'I'll walk you back to your apartment—'

'No!' The sharp exclamation escaped her lips before she could stop it.

'No?' Kahlil queried, his voice turning cold.

His eyes were instantly alert, the formidable mind instantly in gear, Lucy saw with a shiver of apprehension. 'Kahlil, please,' she said, struggling to come up with some excuse. 'I would like to check my plans one last time. There are things I have to be sure of before our next meeting,' she improvised desperately.

'Business can wait,' Kahlil informed her. 'I set the meetings, and therefore I can delay them if I wish. If you need more time, you only have to ask.'

She had to tell him, Lucy realised. He would find out sooner or later. Better she told him than anyone else. 'I have to go back now,' she explained, hearing her voice hoarse with apprehension, 'because I'm not alone—'

'Not alone?' he cut across her harshly. 'What are you talking about?'

'I have a child with me,' Lucy said, and then, bracing herself, she added, 'My son.'

'Your son!' Now it was Kahlil's turn to be completely thrown.

For a moment there was absolute silence. Lucy was frightened when Kahlil refused to look at her, but just stared over her head. She could feel his shock—and, when his shock began subsiding, his mounting suspicion.

This was the price he must pay for trusting her—and for delegating the competition to one of his advisors, Kahlil raged inwardly. Must he oversee everything personally? Clearly, yes! he concluded, raking Lucy with a look. A son! She had never said anything about a child. What type of woman was she?

Suddenly he couldn't wait to get away from her. He needed time to think, to rationalise his feelings, to decide on his next move. 'Go to him, then,' he ordered harshly. 'Go to your son!'

'His name is Edward,' Lucy said quietly as every ounce of her maternal defence mechanism sprang into action. It was terrible to hear Edward spoken about with such anger—and by Kahlil. 'My son's name is Edward,' she said again clearly.

She saw she had Kahlil's full attention now. His eyes were narrowed with distrust. But was it the fact that she had a son alone, or was it her forthrightness? She doubted anyone had ever interrupted Kahlil in his life before. But then perhaps he had never encountered a mother in defence of her child.

Snapping his gaze away from her, Kahlil tried to come to terms with Lucy's startling revelation. As a general rule, he actively encouraged expats working in Abadan to bring their families with them. A happy worker was a good worker, and nothing led to discontent more quickly than homesickness, or the longing for those you loved. The same applied to Lucy. If she had a child, then of course she should have brought him with her. What he took issue with was the manner in which she had kept the information from him. What else was she hiding?

'There is a good play scheme here in the palace, for children of my staff,' he said, turning to her, 'as well as a school…'

Lucy didn't hear any more. Had she joined his staff? Was that how he saw her? Perhaps there was a vacancy for a mistress—

She must keep her head if she was ever to return home safely with Edward. She waited until she was sufficiently composed to say, 'Edward's a little too young for a play scheme, but thank you.'

The words hung in the air between them like an accusation.

'How old is the child?

Kahlil's words plunged like a dagger into Lucy's heart. She couldn't bring herself to answer his question. 'Will you let me go to him?' she said instead, softly.

'Go,' Kahlil said, gesturing impatiently towards the doors.

Kahlil watched her fumbling with the heavy gold handles, not bothering to wait for the servants to open the doors in her haste to get away from him. He did nothing to help, just stood in silence. He would do nothing to aid her path to damnation. He didn't need to. She was doing very well on her own.

It was already dusk by the time Lucy returned to her own rooms at the palace. She was weak with relief after fleeing from Kahlil, and seeing how happily Edward had settled in to his new surroundings almost made her believe that things might be all right after all.

'He woke up soon after you left,' Leila told her, 'but he's been absolutely fine.'

'There are so many new distractions, I'm not surprised,' Lucy murmured, seeking reassurance in Edward's comforting warmth as she lifted him into her arms. But she couldn't compete with this, she realised, looking around. More things had been brought out for him to play with: chalkboards, paints, a wooden train set, toy cars, and even a rocking horse that he was struggling to push Leila away from now that he had mastered the way to ride it.

'I'm afraid he's quite determined to ride it on his own,' Leila explained, 'without me holding on to him. You must be keen on riding,' she added, when Lucy came to take her place in the firing line.

'Yes, I am,' Lucy murmured distractedly, helping Edward to settle back onto the saddle again.

'Or perhaps he takes after his father,' Leila commented, smiling. Then, seeing the look on Lucy's face, she quickly said, 'I'm sorry—I mean—'

'It doesn't matter,' Lucy broke in, reassuring the younger woman with a smile. 'You're probably right, as it happens.'

Leila's comment brought home to her the fact that she didn't know anything about Edward's father. The thought frightened her. But it did seem likely that Kahlil would ride as well as he did everything else. He was built for sport, for action—

Lucy refocused, seeing Leila was still watching her. 'Where did all these things come from?' she said, hoping to deflect the young girl's curiosity.

Leila's eyes widened. 'Apparently this was Sheikh Kahlil's nursery when he was a child,' she confided. 'The servants told me that lots of things had been kept in storage.'

Sheikh Kahlil—*my lover! Edward's father!* Even the way Leila spoke his name with such awe brought the perils of her situation home to Lucy.

'Everyone in the palace has been so kind,' Leila carried on happily, oblivious to the turmoil spinning around Lucy's head. 'The older servants told me that it was good to have a baby around the palace again—Are you all right?' she said, breaking off.

'Yes, I'm fine, thank you. I'm absolutely fine,' Lucy said, managing a thin smile. She was anything but. She was recognising that this was Edward's rightful heritage—all this attention, all this luxury, this was the privileged lifestyle she was denying her son. How could she not tell Edward about Abadan? He must learn about his second country. How could she let him grow to maturity never knowing the truth—that Sheikh Kahlil, the heir to the kingdom of Abadan, was his father?

But if she told Kahlil they had a son together, he would think she had some ulterior motive. Why else would she have kept the news of their child from him for so long? Being so rich and powerful meant Kahlil must harbour suspicions about everyone. How would he feel about a woman who turned up with a young child, claiming he was his son? And what if Kahlil took it into his head to send her away and keep Edward with him in Abadan?

In spite of Edward's protests, Lucy swept her son off the rocking horse and hugged him close. There was not going to be an easy answer, an easy solution. She would just have to get them both out of Abadan somehow, and seek legal advice when she got back.

'You must hear this.'

Lucy turned as Leila distracted her.

'We were recording some tunes,' Leila explained, 'so the children in the playgroup could sing "Happy Birthday" to Edward at his tea party tomorrow. Edward grabbed the microphone—'

As Leila turned on the machine Lucy had to admit the improvement in the clarity of his few words was marked. He had even tried to speak a word or two in Abadanese. But she was used to changes coming thick and fast now. She could hardly keep up with them. He had been able to take a few steps for some time, as long as something or someone supported him. And Kahlil had missed everything.

Guilt speared through Lucy as she thought of it. And then there was something far worse. She felt Kahlil enter the room. She didn't even need to turn around to know he was there. An icy hand slithered down her spine. Edward was staring unblinking at the door. And then Kahlil must have made some signal she could not see, for, without uttering a word, Leila hurried past her out of the room.

'Kahlil!' Lucy's grip on Edward tightened as she turned around to face him.

'Strange,' he said, coming closer. 'I imagined an older child. Now, why did I think that?'

Lucy's throat dried. She wasn't sure if an answer was expected of her. And when Kahlil was cloaked in formal Arabian robes, as he was now, she found the sight of him utterly terrifying. They gave him such grandeur, as well as an untouchable quality that made him seem like a stranger. And in many ways he was. Dressed head to foot in black, unrelieved apart from the gold *agal* that held his headdress in place, he was certainly a formidable figure, with his dark complexion and harsh, unyielding face. But, far from being terrified, Lucy noticed that Edward was transfixed, and didn't flinch or hide his face as the tall, robed figure bore down on them.

Instinctively Lucy took a step backwards, but the moment Kahlil was in reach Edward shot out a hand, and to her surprise Kahlil allowed him to wrap his chubby fist around one of his long, tanned fingers.

'I am very pleased to meet you, Edward,' Kahlil politely, letting the boy hang on to him.

Lucy's heart was hammering as she watched her son's reaction to his father. His eyes wore the same determined expression as Kahlil's. And, just like Kahlil, his unblinking expression seemed incapable of showing fear.

'I was just going to give him a bath,' Lucy said, starting to turn away.

'Not so fast,' Kahlil said, catching hold of her arm. 'How old is this child?'

'Edward…Edward is almost one. Tomorrow is his birthday,' Lucy said, tilting her chin to stare Kahlil in the eyes.

'Is he mine?'

She had not anticipated a question half so blunt. As Lucy tensed she felt Edward tense too.

'I asked you, is he my child?'

Kahlil delivered the words in a merciless staccato sequence, not loud enough to alarm Edward, but chilling to Lucy. The evidence was there in front of his eyes, how

could she deny it? There was no mistaking the fact that
Kahlil was Edward's father; the likeness between them was
uncanny.

'Do we have to do this in front of him?' she said. Edward
was finding the whole situation fascinating, but Lucy knew
there were too many raw emotions in the air, and she wanted
to protect him at all costs from the anger that could erupt
at any second between Kahlil and herself.

A variety of emotions charged across Kahlil's face: tension, enchantment with Edward, then suspicion, and finally
fury. 'Why didn't you tell me?'

'Please, Kahlil—'

But he strode away from her and tugged on a silken rope
to call the servants.

Leila must have been hovering outside, Lucy realised,
waiting for just such a summons. The young girl hesitated
on the threshold, and then came hurrying forwards.

'You called for me?' she said, bobbing respectfully to
Kahlil.

'Yes. Will you take Edward for his bath now, please?'
Kahlil asked, dipping his head to indicate that she should
remove the child from Lucy's arms.

'Of course,' Leila whispered, with another bow.

'And then leave us alone,' Kahlil instructed. 'Miss
Benson will come to collect her son when we have finished
our meeting.'

Lucy's blood ran cold as she passed a reluctant Edward
over to the nanny. Kahlil made the exchange to come between them sound so innocent and clear-cut.

'Go with her now,' Kahlil said directly to Edward, 'and
I will come to see you later.'

Lucy felt a rush of resentment at the way Kahlil had cut
her out. She wanted Edward to protest, to kick up a fuss;
he did neither. He simply locked gazes with his father and
quietened immediately.

'I'll look after him. Don't worry,' Leila assured her, as if sensing Lucy's unease.

But there was an acute sense of threat hovering around Lucy that couldn't be appeased by Leila's reassurances. It was almost as if Edward was going for good, She battled the apprehension raging inside her, but it was all she could do to watch Leila carry Edward across the room without going after them. She had no reason to doubt the nanny, or think the young girl might run off with him. But the dangerous undercurrents in the nursery made Lucy doubt her ability to control anything in Abadan.

Her best course of action was to confront the situation calmly, and find out how Kahlil intended to proceed before doing anything.

As the door clicked shut behind Leila and Edward the room seemed ominously quiet. The quiet before the storm, Lucy thought, mentally preparing herself.

Kahlil's voice split the silence like a blade. 'Why have you brought the child here?'

Lucy stared at up him, holding her ground. 'You know why. I'm working here—I have a contract—'

'Have you come to Abadan to extort money out of me?'

'I have come here to do a job, and that is all,' she said. 'The only money I expect to be paid in Abadan is the money that is owing to me.'

'Well, you won't be getting that yet,' Kahlil said stonily. 'You haven't completed the contract. And you may never complete it.'

Was he threatening her? Trying to drive her away? Lucy's face darkened. 'I can't believe you would be so unprofessional.'

'And I can't believe you would bring the child here—a pawn in your sordid game.'

'Edward isn't a pawn in anyone's game,' Lucy said, incensed that Kahlil might think her capable of such a thing.

'He came with me because I'm a single mother, and that's what single mothers do. When their support system falls down, they adapt, they find a way to carry on—'

Kahlil's sound of contempt was meant to wound her, and it did.

'Think what you like of me,' Lucy told him coldly, 'but don't you dare bring Edward into this.'

Kahlil's gaze hardened. No one ever countermanded Sheikh Kahlil of Abadan, or gave him instructions. Lucy saw that at once.

'Can you prove he's mine?'

Lucy went cold, and for a moment she couldn't think what to say. In that instant she saw herself through Kahlil's eyes. It was obvious what kind of woman he thought she was, and every protective instinct she possessed reared up in defence of her son. 'Prove he's yours?' she said with disdain. 'Why on earth should I want to?'

Kahlil gave a short, ugly laugh. 'I would have thought that was obvious.'

'Not to me, I'm afraid,' Lucy said. 'I can give Edward everything he will ever need. I don't need you.'

'Oh, really?' Kahlil observed softly. 'That's not what you said to me once.'

The sharp reminder of their one night of passion sent a clear message. He thought she was an opportunist who seized the moment when it suited her. And in some ways he was right. She had been vulnerable then—at her lowest ebb. And in those few ecstatic hours, yes, she had needed him.

'What do you hope to gain from this?'

'Nothing,' Lucy assured him. 'And that's a low thing to say, Kahlil. It's not worthy, even of you. I don't want anything—how many times do I have to tell you that? As far as I'm concerned you can cancel my contract—'

'And allow you to leave Abadan with the job half finished and a child who might be my son?'

'It's good to see you've got your priorities straight,' Lucy said tensely. 'The contract first, your son second!'

'My son?' Kahlil repeated softly.

The blood drained out of Lucy's face. His presence of mind at the critical moment had allowed him to uncover the truth. 'I won't stay here,' she whispered.

'You'll do whatever I tell you to do.'

'I'll call the Embassy—'

'Call away,' Kahlil invited, glancing down at a telephone on the table. 'It will do you no good. A simple paternity test will establish whether or not I am Edward's father. And if the test proves positive no embassy on earth will dare to come between me and my son.'

'But you don't even know him,' Lucy said. 'You don't know Edward at all!'

'We have made a very good start,' Kahlil observed coolly. 'I see no reason why we cannot grow even closer—'

'But I'm his mother,' Lucy interjected. 'You can't take him away from me.'

'This is my country,' Kahlil said calmly, 'and here in Abadan my word is law. My people support me in everything I do. They trust me. If they hear that I have a son they will be overjoyed, and he will never be allowed to leave the country—unless, of course, I agree to it.'

He wanted Lucy to be hurt as he had been hurt, Kahlil realised, hearing himself land blow after verbal blow. But he had been staggered by the child's likeness to him. Edward was a true Saeed Al-Sharif. With or without the test, he knew his firstborn was in the palace now. It was a life-changing moment. Edward would one day inherit the throne of Abadan.

Lucy Benson had denied him the chance to know his son. How could such a betrayal go unpunished? She had denied him a whole year of Edward's life…a whole year when he hadn't even known of his son's existence. He would never forgive her for that.

'So, what are you saying?' Lucy demanded.

'If Edward proves to be my son he will stay in Abadan, with or without you.'

'No!' she said, shaking her head in disbelief. 'If you cared for Edward at all, you wouldn't say such a thing.'

'If Edward is my son I should have the chance to care for him as much as you!'

Their voices were raised, and anger crackled in the air as they confronted each other head-on. Neither one of them heard the door open.

'Oh, I'm sorry,' Leila said, hovering on the threshold. 'I forgot something for Edward.'

Hearing their son's name, both Kahlil and Lucy turned around at the same moment.

As they stared at him, Edward frowned, and then quite suddenly erupted into noisy, heart-wrenching sobs.

CHAPTER FIVE

LUCY woke herself up the next morning thrashing about on the bed. For one brief moment she was totally elated, knowing it was Edward's birthday, but then she remembered the previous day's events. They came pouring into her waking mind, leaving no room for happy thoughts, crushing her beneath the fear of what Kahlil might do.

She was in danger, Lucy realised, and, worse, she had put Edward in danger. When he had begun to cry the previous evening she had felt the same fierce and protective instinct she always experienced where any threat to him was concerned. But this time she had seen something similar in Kahlil's face. They had both hurried across to comfort him, but for the first time ever Edward had turned away from her, burrowing his face into Leila's chest instead. Wheeling on his heels, Kahlil had left them as silently as he had arrived. But the look in his eyes would stay with her for ever. It frightened her. Instead of this being one of the happiest days of her life, as she had always imagined it would be, she had never felt more alone, or more vulnerable.

Lucy swung out of bed, knowing the tap at the door heralded the arrival of a breakfast tray. Under other circumstances it might have been a welcome distraction, but with a few short words of thanks Lucy waved it away. The last thing she felt like was eating. She had settled Edward into the adjoining nursery at bedtime, staying with him until he was asleep, and she wanted to be the first to greet him on this, his special day.

She had left the door between their rooms slightly ajar, fearing the worst, without knowing what the worst might be. At one point she had even contemplated bringing Edward into her own bed, to be sure of him, but he had been sleeping so soundly she hadn't liked to wake him. Now she could hear him crowing with delight, as he always did when the sun shone brightly. And the sun always shone in Abadan, Lucy realised tensely as she hurried across the room.

Reaching the nursery, Lucy swept Edward into her arms, taking pleasure and comfort from his innocent baby scent. Just holding him close and feeling his warmth seemed to renew her strength and determination. She turned to cross to the windows and draw back the heavy curtains properly, then made a small sound of shock when she saw Kahlil standing in the shadows by the door, arms folded, watching her.

'Good morning, Lucy.'

She stood frozen, immobile, aware that at the sound of his father's voice Edward's level of excitement had increased. And now he was reaching out, leaning across, making it difficult for her to hold him.

'Shall I take him?'

Before she could reply Edward was taken from her arms, and she watched as Kahlil lifted him high above his head. She saw identical dark brown eyes lock and laugh together, and the identical sweep of thick black lashes cast shadows over olive skin. They were a pair, father and son, interchangeable, their faces so similar that Edward might have been Kahlil at a younger age. The realisation chilled Lucy as she watched them. And the look in Kahlil's eyes chilled her even more. As far as he was concerned she was a nothing, a nobody—just someone standing on the sidelines watching as Kahlil ben Saeed Al-Sharif laid claim to his son.

There was no time to lose, Lucy realised as Edward ran the tip of one finger curiously down the folds of Kahlil's

flowing black headdress. She had to take Edward away from
Abadan. But it would be difficult and dangerous.

Dressed for riding, in a tight fitting black polo shirt, dun-
coloured breeches and boots, Kahlil looked every bit the
desert prince, the warrior prince, and Lucy's stomach
clenched with apprehension as he stared at her. Tilting her
chin at a defiant angle, she stared right back. In spite of the
way her body insisted on responding to him, she would not
weaken—not where her son was concerned. Kahlil might
think every woman could be bent to his will, but he was
about to learn that, in her case at least, they could not.

Escape from Abadan—the thought chilled her to the mar-
row. But what alternative did she have? She had to make
plans before matters were taken out of her hands entirely.
Whatever the risks, she would not lose Edward.

She would not lose her son.

Leila's arrival, and the routine she automatically put into
action, left Kahlil and Lucy with little to do other than stand
tensely as the young nanny swept Edward off for his morning bath. Lucy was relieved when Kahlil left the room then,
without a word or a backward glance. There was no reason
for him to stay now, and with Edward gone, and a business
meeting later that morning, Lucy left for her own quarters.

Calling in one last time, to say goodbye to Edward before
her meeting, Lucy found the nursery alive with activity.
Edward was dressed in Arab dress and sitting happily on
his play mat. He looked so different. And yet there was
nothing wrong with Leila dressing him in the local costume,
Lucy told herself; it was cooler for him.

Edward was so happily engaged with the presents in front
of him that, once again, he barely noticed her. Normally she
wouldn't have taken it to heart, but today was different. This
was Kahlil's doing, Lucy realised indignantly. He had made
a point of coming back to the nursery before her and show-
ering Edward with far too many gifts. She would not have

Edward growing up spoiled and arrogant like his father, careless of other people's feelings. Resentment reared up inside her, but she forced it down quickly when Leila came towards her across the room. None of this was the young girl's fault.

'I'll save this until after the meeting,' Lucy said, placing her own carefully wrapped parcel on the table. 'Please don't let Edward open it until I come back.'

But Edward was far too preoccupied with a box containing a toy Lamborghini to even notice he had yet another package to open.

'Of course I won't,' Leila said, glancing at her charge. 'Sheikh Kahlil came by,' she added, 'with lots of presents.'

'So I see,' Lucy said dryly. 'Don't worry, you've done nothing wrong,' she said, seeing the concern on Leila's face. 'Edward's going to have a great birthday. Everyone has been so kind.' But poor Leila looked more dubious than ever. 'Well, at least Edward's happy, and that's all that matters,' Lucy said firmly, moving away to escape the younger woman's scrutiny.

Picking her son up, she hid her face in his baby warmth for a few moments. 'And now there's a party to organise,' she said brightly, pulling back. 'What is it, Leila?' she added, turning when she heard the nanny's muted exclamation. 'What's wrong?'

'I'm really sorry, but—'

'Go on,' Lucy prompted.

'When Sheikh Kahlil came back to the nursery he was accompanied by one of his aides. He left instructions that you weren't to concern yourself with the party. He said he would make all the arrangements for Edward's birthday.'

'Did he indeed?' Lucy murmured tensely.

'It will be fantastic,' Leila said reassuringly.

'I'm sure it will be,' Lucy said, releasing Edward onto his mat again. 'I'll make sure of it.'

Lucy saw the look of concern that settled on Leila's face, but she was determined to have some input into Edward's first birthday party. Kahlil had no official part to play in Edward's life—not yet.

She gazed around at the piles of expensive gifts. Kahlil must have rung the nearest toy shop and had everything appropriate to Edward's age delivered to the palace. He was already sure Edward was his son! But proof would be needed, Lucy realised, feeling a stab of fear. 'Did anyone touch Edward while I was away?'

'No, of course not,' Leila said. 'Except—'

'Yes?' Lucy pressed tensely.

'Sheikh Kahlil played with him, of course, and lifted him up.'

Leila's innocent account was very frightening to Lucy. 'And Edward was OK with that?'

'Of course,' Leila said promptly. 'Edward loves Sheikh Kahlil.' Seeing Lucy's expression, she amended quickly, 'What I mean is, Sheikh Kahlil makes him laugh.'

Lucy forced a smile onto her face. 'But no one else touched him? You're sure?' The possibility of a DNA test being carried out without her permission was niggling at her mind.

'No, of course not,' Leila said adamantly. 'You know I wouldn't let anyone near Edward—apart from the Sheikh.' But she still looked very worried as she held Lucy's stare.

Leila was wondering what on earth she had got herself into, Lucy realised. 'I don't mean to criticise you,' she said quickly. 'It's just that we're in a strange country, and I have to be sure in my mind that Edward is safe.'

'I understand, and I won't ever leave him alone.'

'I believe you,' Lucy assured the young nanny gently. 'And maybe I'm being too hasty about that party. The Sheikh's people will surely know where to get everything we need.'

'Absolutely,' Leila agreed, brightening. 'They're even talking about having a funfair for all the children at the palace.'

'That would be fantastic,' Lucy agreed. She felt a little better knowing that Edward's birthday provided an excuse for a general celebration where everyone would have fun.

'Shall I take Edward, so that you can prepare for your meeting?' Leila suggested.

'I'm ready now—but what I'd really like is a few minutes alone with him—if you don't mind?'

'Of course I don't mind,' Leila said, touching her arm lightly.

The kindly gesture brought tears rushing to Lucy's eyes. She blinked them away quickly, before Leila saw. But she sensed the young girl already knew there was something very wrong.

Lucy was glad of the meeting, to discuss the design project in depth. It was a complete change of pace, and one she badly needed.

Everything went smoothly in the Council Chamber, where Kahlil behaved as if there was nothing between them other than business. He even made it possible for her to go through the agenda quickly, as if he too was in a rush to get away. And when the meeting drew to a close he left the room before she even had time to tidy up her papers.

She felt the tension starting to drain out of her the moment the door closed behind him. She was in good time to help prepare for the birthday celebrations. All she had to do was change into something more suitable for a children's party.

Lucy stood amazed at the top of a sweeping flight of marble steps overlooking the palace garden. A huge part of the grounds had been transformed into a fairground, with stalls and a skittle alley, and even a full-sized carousel, all shielded from the sun by giant-sized marquees. Clowns walked about on stilts, distributing flags and streamers to the crowds of children with their parents and teachers, and hurdy-gurdy music blasted out from several speakers. Where money was no object, anything was possible, she realised.

She had changed into jeans, sneakers and a blue gingham shirt, ready for action. Just as well, since many of the rides were suitable for Edward. At the moment he was sitting patiently in his buggy, by her side, but she knew his apparent contentment was misleading and wouldn't last long.

The marquees were air-conditioned, Lucy discovered when she wheeled Edward inside the largest tent.

'Sheikh Kahlil thinks of everything,' Leila commented.

'Yes, he does,' Lucy said—though whether that was a good thing… 'I hardly know where to start first,' she murmured, looking around.

'How about the carousel?'

Lucy jumped with shock at the sound of Kahlil's voice. She had been so sure he would not be there. At the meeting earlier he had given her the impression that he had somewhere important to go; a children's party was the last thing she had imagined. He was casually dressed in jeans, and a shirt rolled up to the elbows—just like the first time they'd met. It was a painful reminder. Gazing up, transfixed, Lucy found she could hardly breathe, barely speak.

'Well?' Kahlil said.

'Well, what?' Lucy queried distractedly. And then she realised he wasn't speaking to her at all, but to Edward. And Edward was holding out his arms, waiting for Kahlil to lift him up.

Dipping down to sweep his son out of the pushchair, Kahlil lifted him high in the air. Lucy saw his mouth settle in a look of supreme pride and satisfaction, and then, settling him on his shoulders, he walked off.

Sheikh or no sheikh, bodyguards or whatever else might stand in her way, Lucy wasn't going to let Kahlil get away with that. Pushing through the crowds, she had almost caught up with him when security men stepped in front of her, barring her way.

'Let her pass.' Kahlil's voice was low, but commanding, and they backed off immediately.

'You can't do this, Kahlil,' Lucy said tensely. 'You can't just take Edward away from me without a word of explanation.'

Glancing up to reassure himself that Edward was too busy watching the painted horses to notice the tension, Kahlil speared a look at her. 'And you can't stop me getting to know this boy any longer—a boy who is probably my son.'

'Don't you think you're getting a little ahead of yourself?'

'Am I? There is only one way to resolve this beyond doubt,' he said, settling Edward in front of him on one of the carousel ponies.

'And what is that?' Lucy said tensely, glad that Edward was too excited to notice the high-octane discussion being carried out in murmurs above his head.

'We will have a DNA test carried out.'

'No!' Lucy had known it would come to this. But she'd wanted it to happen away from Abadan, where she might have some control over the repercussions. 'Don't spoil his birthday—please, Kahlil,' she begged. 'Please, just drop it for today.'

Fleetingly, Kahlil looked as if he might consider her appeal, and Lucy's hopes soared. She didn't want to deny Kahlil the right to know his son, or keep Edward from his father. She just wanted a little more time. But then the raucous music started up again and she was left alone, while Kahlil and Edward began moving slowly away from her.

*   *   *

He had forgotten that it was possible to have so much innocent fun, Kahlil thought wryly as the carousel came to a halt at the end of the ride. It was a relaxation for him to be just one of many adults taking their small children for a ride on the gaudy machine. He felt elated. He had felt nothing quite like it before.

He gritted his jaw, seeing Lucy was still standing where they had left her. There was no question in his mind about Edward; they were uncannily alike. He glanced around, wondering if anyone else had noticed. But his bond with the child went deeper than appearance, Kahlil reflected, getting ready to dismount; there was real chemistry between them. And their character was identical, he noticed with amusement, when Edward refused to get down from his perch.

'Perhaps later,' he consoled the determined child. 'Your mother is waiting for you now.'

Seeing Lucy's face, Kahlil felt something close to pity. She looked so fearful, so tense and anxious. He brushed the emotion aside, remembering that she had kept him from a child he was increasingly sure now was his son. Fate had stepped in for him; fate had brought them together in spite of her deception. He had nothing to thank Lucy Benson for. Still…

'Edward will not be touched without your consent,' he told her. 'But a DNA test will be necessary. Accept it.'

Lowering Edward to the ground, Kahlil supported him as he took a few bold steps towards his pushchair. 'Soon you'll be walking by yourself,' he commented, hunkering down so his face was on a level with Edward's.

White-faced, Lucy moved between them, and secured Edward back in the stroller herself.

Let her have this victory, Kahlil told himself, waving his bodyguards away. Lucy's breach of etiquette meant that men who remained otherwise invisible, mingling with the crowds, instantly surrounded him. They were always alert for danger, but he would not allow them to restrain Lucy now, or at any other time. Whatever she had done to deceive him, she was still the mother of his son.

The mother of his son! Kahlil felt as if his heart would burst with pride. Edward: his son. He ran the child's name over in his mind, loving the sound of it. Lucy might not have admitted as much as yet, but she would not be allowed to leave Abadan until he had formally established the truth of Edward's parentage.

CHAPTER SIX

THIS would be her third full day in Abadan, and instead of improving things for Edward she had thrown his future into confusion, Lucy reflected, tossing restlessly on the bed.

And now it was time to get up, she saw, checking the clock on the bedside table.

She groaned as she swung her legs over the side of the bed, and stayed slumped with her head almost touching her knees, her long golden hair tickling her calves. She had checked on Edward so many times during the night she felt as if she hadn't slept at all. The belief that Kahlil would never snatch him from her was no consolation. She couldn't escape the thought that one day Edward would choose Abadan, and Kahlil, over her, and it frightened her.

Sensibly, the only thing she could do was get him away from Kahlil and out of the country as fast as possible. Once she was home she could arrange with a lawyer to see that Edward shared his time between them—but even that wouldn't be right, Lucy thought, lifting her head to stare blindly into the future. Even that would not be enough for a man like Sheikh Kahlil ben Saeed Al-Sharif of Abadan.

She had to get away. It was all that was left to her now. She knew what she had to do, but she had to find the right opportunity to put her plan into action.

Hurrying into the nursery, Lucy smiled down at her son, waiting impatiently, arms raised, to be freed from his cot. If they remained in Abadan it meant complying with every restriction Kahlil cared to throw at them—and she was never going to let that happen.

'Never, my darling,' she assured Edward, swinging him into the air.

There was deep tension inside the robing room of the Sheikh of Abadan.

'Leave us,' Kahlil's father commanded his courtiers imperiously.

Age might have imposed certain restrictions upon him, most onerous of which was the indignity of the stout ebony stick he was now forced to use, but Kahlil thrilled to hear his father's voice still firm and as commanding as ever. He watched the bowing courtiers back out of the opulent chamber, and waited until the door had closed behind them before turning to speak to the ruler of Abadan.

'I wanted to be the one to tell you before any gossip reached your ears,' he said, after explaining about Edward.

'If you have the slightest suspicion regarding the child's parentage he must be brought here at once,' his father said, his black eyes sharp as a hawk's above his aquiline nose. 'For his own safety, Kahlil, if nothing else. If this should get out—'

'I am confident that no one else knows about this as yet.'

'As yet,' his father observed. 'You say the likeness between you is uncanny? In your heart I believe you already know the truth.'

'I cannot be certain—'

'Until the test is done,' his father pointed out.

'You must allow me to handle this,' Kahlil said firmly. 'Lucy would never agree to a test being carried out here in Abadan. She does not trust us.'

'I take it you are referring to the mother?' The old Sheikh shook his head, seeing the irony of the situation. But he also saw his son's unbending will clearly reflected in his eyes.

And there was more—enough to arouse his suspicion that emotion was involved. Emotion clouded judgement. He would act on his son's behalf if he had to. 'There is something about this situation you are not telling me,' he observed shrewdly.

'There is nothing more,' Kahlil said dismissively.

But some internal pain as real as any wound flickered behind Kahlil's eyes, and his father knew at once what he must do.

Back in his own rooms, before meeting later that morning with Lucy, Kahlil sat with his chin on his hand, staring fiercely into the future. He had the look about him of a man who truly believed he could bend it to his will.

Adopting Edward as his heir would not be a simple matter, as his father seemed to imagine. The ruling Sheikh had lived through an age when women could be swept up and cast down again as required—though Kahlil had to smile, remembering his own mother. She had not been swept up, or cast down. If anything, his father had been the one to lose his heart, as well as his stubborn adherence to tradition, when they met.

And now there was Lucy Benson. She was hardly doormat material either. She was the very antithesis of a willing woman—in all ways but one, Kahlil remembered, feeling his senses stir. She was headstrong, unpredictable, and outrageously provocative. But did he want a woman who gave herself to a man within the first minutes of their meeting? Not to sit beside him on the throne of Abadan one day, that was for sure. Lucy Benson was not good wife material, and certainly inconceivable as consort to the eventual ruler of Abadan—but there was nothing to stop him taking her as his mistress.

A pact, Kahlil concluded finally, standing and stretching to his full height so that his shadow cast a menacing shade across the wall. There would have to be an accommodation between them. Edward would stay in Abadan, while the best minds in the land would examine the law to see if his son could be named as his legitimate heir without marriage to his mother. In the fullness of time he would select someone more suited to sit beside him on the throne.

Kahlil's lips turned down at the thought. He knew it couldn't be one of the relentlessly acquiescent women whom his father paraded before him in the hopes that eventually he might bite. They were all glassy-eyed at the thought of his power and wealth. Not one of them had been able to tempt him beyond the bedroom. As far as he was concerned they were despicable creatures—toys to be used and discarded, as they would have used him.

His expression darkened as he strode towards the door. He had better things to think about. Edward and Lucy had been placed under a discreet protection programme from the first moment his suspicions had been roused. That would have to be stepped up now, but the child would stay with his mother for the time being.

This meeting had been the best so far, Lucy thought with relief as she hurried back to the nursery. Whether she felt so good because without Kahlil there had been no tension, or whether it was just the fact that things were going so well, either way her confidence was high. For the first time she really believed she could handle the situation—

Lucy's breath caught in her throat as she reached the end of the corridor. She could feel the change even before her eyes had registered anything. Instinctively she began to run, but someone leapt out of the shadows and barred her way.

With a yelp of fright, she stopped abruptly. A tall man in dark clothes loomed over her—and he was carrying what looked like a gun.

'Edward!'

The guttural scream leapt from Lucy's throat as she tried

to shoulder past him. But the man, having caught hold of her, wouldn't let go.

'The Sheikh of Abadan,' Lucy panted, almost beside herself with fright. 'I demand to see the Sheikh!' Whether or not it was something in her voice that shook him, she had no idea, but he released her. And then she saw Leila, peering anxiously round the partially open nursery door. 'Leila, thank God! Where's Edward?'

'He's in here,' Leila said quickly, drawing her inside. 'Edward is safe.'

Lucy slammed the door behind her, leaning against it as she fought to catch her breath, and saw Edward safe inside his playpen, playing unconcerned. Shutting her eyes, she gave a soft cry of relief. 'Who ordered this?' she said, hurrying over to him.

'Sheikh Kahlil,' Leila said unhappily.

Lucy's mouth formed a firm white line. 'And where is Sheikh Kahlil now?'

'I don't know,' the girl admitted.

'Then we must ask his guard,' Lucy declared fiercely. Swinging the door open again, she called him in.

She rounded on the man the moment he entered the room, demanding fiercely, 'Sheikh Kahlil? Where is he? You'd better tell me.'

But the man only shook his head and shrugged his shoulders.

'I have a few words of Abadanese. Do you mind if I try?' Leila offered.

'No, please—go right ahead,' Lucy urged.

After a few minutes had passed Leila was able to tell her that Kahlil had gone to his stud farm as soon as he was satisfied that additional security was in place at the nursery.

The noose was tightening, Lucy realised. Soon everyone would know about Edward. Even without a parentage test Kahlil wasn't taking any chances, and the people around him weren't fools. It made the need for her to get away from Abadan with Edward all the more pressing. But before she could formulate a plan she had to know exactly what she was up against.

'I must speak to someone about this,' she said, careful not to arouse Leila's suspicions. 'I have to explain that this level of security is unnecessary. Perhaps as Sheikh Kahlil isn't available to talk to me I might have an audience with his father? Can you ask the guard about it?' she said to Leila.

Leila was already shaking her head. 'He's not like his son.' She frowned. 'He comes from a different age, a different world—I don't even know if he would agree to see you.'

'Please—do this for me,' Lucy insisted. 'This is outrageous,' she pointed out, flaring a look at the armed guard. 'I have to speak to someone—it must be possible!'

Lucy took time choosing what she would wear for her audience with the ruling Sheikh of Abadan. Despite her bravado she could hardly believe he had agreed to see her. She had rehearsed what she would say, and how she would say it, over and over, to make sure there would be no hesitation on her part—and no mistakes. She should get it right; she'd had enough time to practise her lines, she thought, glancing at her wristwatch for the umpteenth time. She had been kept waiting in the antechamber to Kahlil's father's rooms for hours. It was now early evening.

'Miss Benson?'

Lucy looked up to see the Sheikh's aide-de-camp had returned at last. He was beckoning to her from an open doorway.

'Thank you,' Lucy said, getting to her feet and quickly walking past him before he had a chance to change his mind. Perhaps she had been kept waiting in order to take the wind of righteous indignation out of her sails before the interview. Well, if that was so, it hadn't worked.

Kahlil's father was seated on a chair at the far end of the ornately decorated room. Sitting stiffly upright, he was as gnarled as the branches of the olive trees in the courtyard outside her bedroom window, and must be at least eighty, she guessed, as she bowed low in front of him in deference to his age.

'Come closer, so that I can see you in the light,' he instructed.

She saw now that his chair was more of a carved and gilded throne, made comfortable by a mound of velvet cushions. There was a fringed canopy of rich purple velvet above his head, and he looked every bit the old warrior king of Abadan.

Compromise was the way forward, not confrontation, Lucy decided. She could not take on the whole of Abadan and its ruler. She had to play by Abadanese rules—at least while she was in the country. And despite his reputation, and his fierce appearance, there was something courteous about the old gentleman that demanded she respond in kind.

She took a step forward so that she was standing directly beneath a surprisingly old-fashioned standard lamp positioned to one side of him. It cast a soft pool of light on the ruby-red rug beneath her feet, and was completed by a faded fabric shade in a colour that might once have been peach. It looked as if it must have come from some Western department store specialising in luxury goods many years before, and was certainly incongruous in such an exotic setting.

'I see you are interested in my lamp,' the elderly Sheikh commented benignly, his voice firm, if a little hoarse.

He missed nothing, Lucy realised. She would have to proceed with great caution.

'My wife was from the West—why, Miss Benson, you look surprised.'

'No,' Lucy fudged, laughing tensely, though of course she

was. But by the time she had absorbed that piece of information she felt a little calmer because she knew he was trying to make her feel at ease.

'You *are* surprised,' Kahlil's father said with a high-pitched cackle of delight. 'My son has failed to tell you that he straddles the divide between East and West?'

Now was not the right time to admit she knew as little about Kahlil as he knew about her, Lucy realised, making a non-committal sound.

'Won't you be seated?' his father invited, pointing to a similar mound of cushions, minus the throne, facing his own.

Had the ruling Sheikh not told her about Kahlil's heritage, Lucy would have been amazed by this suggestion that she should sit in his presence. 'Thank you,' she said. She sat, trying to judge the right moment to put her case. But Kahlil's father forestalled her.

'And how is my grandson this morning? I am eager to see him.'

Lucy was so taken aback she couldn't summon up a single word in reply.

'You must be pleased that I acknowledge Edward,' the Sheikh of Abadan continued. 'Now you know about Kahlil's heritage, you will understand how I am able to accept a child of Kahlil's who dilutes the Abadanese bloodline.'

Lucy felt like a brood mare, but she was equally sure the elderly Sheikh had not meant to offend her. 'If I may speak—I beg your pardon, Majesty,' she said quickly, 'I did not mean to interrupt you, but I'm sure you can understand my concern for my son.'

'Indeed,' he agreed, inclining his head graciously. 'And, equally, I am sure you can understand *my* concern for my grandson.'

'Aren't you being a little premature?' Lucy parried.

'Are you trying to tell me Edward is not Kahlil's son?'

Lucy reddened beneath the hawk-like stare.

When she remained silent, the elderly Sheikh said, 'You do not have to say anything Miss Benson; I already know the truth.'

'How can you?' Lucy said tensely.

'Quite simply,' he said. 'DNA tests have been carried out—'

'How dare he?'

'Who are you talking about, Miss Benson?'

'Kahlil, of course,' Lucy said angrily, springing to her feet.

'I can see you are upset, but, please, do sit down again.'

'Upset?' Lucy said her lips white with anger. 'That doesn't even begin to cover it! This amounts to an assault on my son as far as I am concerned. I am Edward's mother; nothing should have been done without my consent.'

'I disagree,' the Sheikh told her. 'The responsibility for Edward's welfare has been taken out of your hands—on my command,' he added imperiously, when Lucy started to protest.

Now she could only stare at the elderly man, nonplussed. The Sheikh of Abadan made it sound as if she should be relieved, even grateful to him for relieving her of such a burden! But it was Edward they were talking about—her son Edward!

'As eventual heir to the throne of Abadan,' he continued evenly, 'only we can hope to give Edward all the security and the education he needs before he assumes the mantle of power.'

'No! You cannot take my son away from me. I will not allow it!'

'You have no alternative, Miss Benson. It is a *fait accompli*.'

'You had no right to carry out tests without my permission—'

'This is my country. I will do whatever I consider necessary to protect the boy I have just learned is second in line to my throne.'

Edward, heir to the throne of Abadan! It struck Lucy so forcibly her throat dried. 'You can't—'

'Oh, but I can,' the Sheikh of Abadan told her. 'Here, my word is law.'

'Your word, and that of your son,' Lucy said bitterly.

'Correct, Miss Benson—or may I call you Lucy?'

'I think it better that we confine ourselves to a formal style of address,' Lucy said coldly, knowing that the next time they met was likely to be in court. The DNA testing might be a *fait accompli*, and Kahlil's right to claim Edward as his son something she was forced to accept, but she would not be compromised where her son was concerned, nor allow either of them to be patronised by anyone. 'If no one knows that Edward is Kahlil's son, surely he's not at risk,' she reasoned out loud. 'I will keep him safe.' She turned her burning gaze on the Sheikh. 'Let me have my son back. Let me go home with Edward.'

'I'm afraid it's not as clear cut as that,' he told her patiently. 'Please sit down again.' He waited until she did as he asked. 'Even walls have ears. Palace gossip flourishes. There are no secrets here. Even I would find it impossible to keep this type of information quiet for long.'

'Then let us go—somewhere far away, where Edward will be safe.'

'My son has rights too,' Kahlil's father pointed out. 'Would you deny Edward the chance to know his father? Would you deny your son the right to claim his birthright?'

Silence hung heavily between them as Lucy came to terms with the situation. 'If I went home and left Edward here,' she said at last, in a voice that had lost its bite, 'could you promise to keep him safe?'

'I could,' the elderly Sheikh confirmed in a kinder tone.

'Edward would have the best of everything—everything that money can buy. I promise you that. And of course, as mother of the royal child, you would receive an extremely handsome pension—'

'What?' Lucy exclaimed, springing up again. 'Do you think you can buy me? Forgive me if I misunderstood you,' she said tensely, 'but did you just offer me money in return for my son?'

'Now, now—you mustn't look at it that way—'

'And just how am I supposed to look at it?'

'It is normal in such circumstances,' the Sheikh said calmly, as if there was nothing wrong with his offer at all.

Perhaps it was a regular occurrence in Abadan…perhaps it was a regular occurrence where Kahlil was concerned, Lucy thought. In her distressed state, she would have believed anything possible…or perhaps it was time to put Kahlil out of her mind once and for all, she realised bitterly. That was the safest course of action for Edward, and for her.

'As I see it,' she said, gathering the last vestiges of her strength and determination together, 'the best thing that can happen is that I take Edward home with me to a place where he can live a normal life.'

The Sheikh didn't answer her for a few moments, and then he said, almost as if he had some sympathy for her plight, 'Regrettably, Edward will never be able to live what you think of as a normal life, Miss Benson. He is a royal child. You can never take that away from him. From now on Edward must be taught to handle the weight of responsibility that accompanies privilege.'

'He's one year old!'

'Even so...' The Sheikh of Abadan held out both hands, palm up, in an expression of finality.

Lucy remained silent as all the implications for Edward sank in. From being a happy, carefree little boy, he had been transformed into someone who would require some form of protection for the rest of his life. Could she provide that for him? She doubted it. She needed support in order to do it properly. There was only one person in the world who could offer her that support, and that was Kahlil. Who hadn't even bothered to come back to the palace now that he had secured the gates to her gilded cage! Stick a guard on the door and walk away. That was as far as accepting responsibility for his son went for Kahlil.

The thought of abandoning Edward to that sort of parenting was out of the question. They stayed together. That much she was determined upon. If she could just get them both back home in safety, to be under the protection of her own country's security services…

It was like a madness building inside her; now Lucy could think of nothing else at all—nothing but escape.

CHAPTER SEVEN

'YOU are summoned to a meeting by Sheikh Kahlil ben Saeed Al-Sharif of Abadan.'

'I see. At what time?' Lucy asked the courtier politely. Inwardly she was seething at the nature of the formal summons, but it was hardly the man's fault.

'In one hour,' he said, bowing his way out of the room.

She had been called into Kahlil's presence like a member of his staff, Lucy mused angrily as the door closed; so much for all that empty talk of how she was the mother of the royal child. She was nothing as far as Kahlil and his father were concerned—nothing but an embarrassing encumbrance.

She had sat up half the night after her meeting with Kahlil's father, waiting for Kahlil to return to the palace. And she was still smarting now from the knowledge that someone had sneaked into the nursery to take Edward's hairbrush away. A single hair, she had since learned, was all it took to prove parentage.

She would never have denied Kahlil the chance to know his son. She had just never expected to see the man she'd known as Kahl again. And never in her wildest dreams had she anticipated finding him here in Abadan, heir to the throne of one of the world's richest countries.

Kahlil might be a sheikh, and all-powerful in his own land, but that did not weaken her resolve. She would agree to equal parenting rights, but based on the laws of her own country, not Abadan. To achieve this she had get Edward back home, whatever it took.

Lucy's lips whitened as she thought of the many difficulties she would have to overcome in order to escape. She only had to think of the armed guards on the nursery door to know she was taking a huge risk. But remembering the Sheikh of Abadan's outrageous offer of money in exchange for Edward strengthened her determination. He might be a fine old man, and beloved by his people, but he had no idea how a mother felt in defence of her child. Wherever she went, Edward went too. And she would keep him safe, with or without the help of his royal relatives.

Similar situations must have arisen before, Lucy told herself. There would be ways of dealing with the problem, and people who could advise her once she got back home. But first she had to prepare herself for the meeting with Kahlil. She would deal with business, and then finalise her escape plan. There would never be a better time. Kahlil and his father were convinced she could be bent to their will, manipulated, bought off, sent packing—they were complacent, and now was the time to strike.

And strike she would, Lucy thought fiercely, putting the final touches to her make-up.

Kahlil paced the floor of his royal apartment, hands linked behind his back, in a state of brilliantly controlled fury. His father was like a tiger that could never be tamed. He was forced to admire his pluck, his unquestioned courage, and his determination to rule as if he was still that same warrior king of half a century ago, but there was no question that he had overreached himself this time.

From the moment Kahlil had discovered Edward's DNA had been tested by removing his soft-bristled baby brush from the nursery he had been in a state of simmering fury. It hadn't eased his anger to know that Edward had never been touched. He had given his word to Lucy that nothing would be done without her consent. And his word was his bond. But his father had ridden roughshod over that promise, ordering the test to be carried out regardless of anyone's wishes but his own.

It was indefensible. Edward was a small child, unable to protect himself. His parents should have been consulted—*he* should have been consulted, Kahlil amended swiftly, for he now knew for sure that he was Edward's father.

He turned abruptly as the door opened and Lucy came in. She walked forward, braving a stare that would have stopped many a man in their tracks. But she could not be put off so easily, Kahlil reflected. She finally drew to a halt close enough for him to catch the scent of jasmine. He had to admit she looked beautiful—exquisite. He had never seen her looking so feminine, or so desirable. A muscle worked in his jaw as he wished momentarily that things could have been different between them. But she was white-faced and drawn as taut as a bowstring. This was not a time to be softening towards her.

'Thank you for coming—' he began courteously, but she held up one hand and cut him off.

'Don't even try to explain away the armed guard who steps in front of me every time I try to see my son,' she said crisply. 'And don't waste your time trying to find some excuse for violating Edward's rights. No wonder you avoid seeing me. I'd be apprehensive if I were you—in fact, I'd be scared.'

'Scared?' Kahlil queried icily. He wanted to drag her to him and force her to apologise, but somehow he controlled the impulse. 'I don't know the meaning of that word.' To his utter astonishment, he was forced to catch hold of her striking arm. 'Would you hit me?' he demanded incredulously. 'Would you dare to raise your hand to me?'

Lucy rested still for a moment, panting. She knew she couldn't escape. She knew she had gone too far. 'You don't frighten me, Kahlil.'

'Then you're very foolish.' He turned away from her with

an angry sound, ashamed of rising to the provocation, but knowing he must concede that his father had overstepped the mark. 'There is no excuse for what has happened,' he said, tugging Lucy a little closer for emphasis. 'The only explanation I can give is that Edward's safety is paramount.'

'You promised me,' Lucy said tensely. 'You promised nothing would be done as far as Edward is concerned without my consent.'

She saw Kahlil's gaze sharpen. Could he feel the change in her body as he held her to him? Even while she railed at him Lucy knew she was losing control. Kahlil was the enemy, and yet still she wanted him. It didn't make sense; nothing made sense, Lucy raged inwardly, wrenching out of his grasp. She took a few rapid steps away, rubbing her arms as if he had hurt her. But he had used barely enough force to keep her still. She was just so wretchedly confused.

'The tests were carried out without my knowledge or consent. My father gave the order while I was out of the palace. The people responsible received no contradictory directions from myself—how could they,' Kahlil reasoned, 'when I wasn't there to consult? And therefore they went ahead without my knowledge—'

'I am Edward's mother!' Lucy cut in angrily. 'Why didn't someone come to ask me how I felt about it?'

'Here in Abadan, my father's word is law. And forgive me, Lucy,' Kahlil added, a flash of humour momentarily brightening his gaze, 'but it would never have occurred to my father's servants to consult you, a mere woman.'

'A mere woman,' Lucy repeated, staring up at him coldly. 'I trust you don't feel the same way?' She wondered why his slow smile should make her feel even more anxious and suspicious.

'My father's servants are all from his era. I can assure you they hold very different views to the Abadanese men of today.'

His voice vibrated through her like a soft, harmonious chord: a chord she was determined not to hear. 'And I suppose you consider yourself to be in the latter camp?' Lucy said derisively, but she felt Kahlil's warm breath on her neck bringing all the tiny hairs to attention.

'I do,' he agreed softly.

Lucy broke eye contact fast.

'A single hair from Edward's hairbrush was all that was required,' Kahlil said to reassure her. 'It hardly constitutes an assault.'

'Even so—'

'Enough of that,' he said impatiently, breaking away. 'I asked you to come here so that we could discuss the future of our son. But if you're not interested in hearing what I have to say—'

'Of course I'm interested.'

'Very well. Then why don't we sit down like two civilised people and discuss this calmly?' And then they could continue on smoothly to the subject of Lucy's terms for becoming his mistress, Kahlil mused with satisfaction.

Lucy barely rested on the edge of a hard-backed chair. 'Well?' she prompted. 'What is it you wish to say to me? Though, be warned, I'm in no mood for compromise after the way my trust has been abused.'

'We both want the best for Edward,' Kahlil pointed out. He had imposed a compromise upon his father. Lucy would stay in Abadan. In return she would be allowed to keep Edward. If she refused, Edward would stay without her. The simple solutions were always the best. His people would demand nothing less.

But there was no reason for unpleasantness. He had already determined a way by which she could not only be persuaded to stay, but would do so willingly. And he wanted her to stay, Kahlil knew, feeling his senses quicken at the sight of Lucy's upturned face. Even animated by fury and suspicion she was irresistible. She was consumed by passion, and it had brought a flush to her pale cheeks a flush he would have preferred to impose some other way. He wanted her. He wanted Lucy Benson to stay in Abadan. He wanted her to be his mistress, and to share his bed, but for now...

'Your work has been well received,' he said, skilfully redirecting the conversation. 'There is talk of you doing more.'

'How can you bear to discuss that now?'

'You will be forced to stay here a little longer.'

'Forced?' Lucy repeated tensely. 'I will not be forced to do anything. I will take the return flight I have booked, and return to Abadan as my work here demands. I have other commitments back home.'

'You will not leave until you have finished here,' Kahlil countered. 'You will not forget your commitment to Abadan.'

'Forget?' Lucy said incredulously. 'How can I forget anything about Abadan? How can I forget the fact that I have a son whose father is Sheikh of Abadan? A son who, even now, is behind locked doors with an armed guard standing outside?'

'For his own protection,' Kahlil reminded her.

'And you really think that's the way I want him to live?'

'It is merely a precaution.'

'To protect him from whom?' Lucy said, her voice rising when Kahlil didn't reply. 'No, don't tell me. I already know. There is no danger to the royal family here in Abadan. This country is as stable as it could be. *"The people prosper under the benign reign of the Saeed al-Sharif family,"'* she said, quoting directly from one of the many articles she had read.

'Well done,' Kahlil murmured sardonically.

'I did my homework before I came here, Kahlil,' Lucy

said. 'So please don't try to fob me off with excuses. The only possible danger to Edward would come from outsiders. And as far as you and your father are concerned I am the only outsider in the palace. I can only conclude that you think you're protecting Edward from me!'

She was approaching hysteria, Lucy realised, stopping herself when she heard the panic in her voice. Her cheeks were burning with emotion, and she knew she had already said far too much. Her desperation might put thoughts into Kahlil's head—he might guess she was thinking about escape.

'You're wrong,' he said coldly. 'The fact that I have a son did come as a shock. And the implications for any son of mine are immense. Let me finish,' he insisted, when Lucy started to interrupt. 'As for my father, his reaction was typical of his generation. Things were very different in his day. He was as shocked as I was to learn he has a grandson. The guards make him feel comfortable—'

'Comfortable?' Lucy shook her head in amazement, wondering how anyone could find armed guards comforting.

'He is only trying to protect Edward. It's his way of showing he accepts him into the family.'

Ice ran through Lucy at the implications of that. She felt as if she was hanging on to Edward by her fingertips whilst a whole army of Saeed Al-Sharifs pulled him the other way.

'We both want the best for Edward,' Kahlil said, reclaiming her attention.

It was ironic. They were going to discuss Edward's future, the one thing that joined them, and yet she had never felt greater distance between them. 'Yes,' Lucy agreed tensely, 'we do.'

Deftly arranging his robes, Kahlil sat stiffly facing her. 'You shall have complete freedom while you are in Abadan.'

'Freedom?' Lucy repeated faintly. All her life she had

taken her freedom for granted. She realised now how precious it was.

'You will, of course, have a bodyguard with you at all times.'

'Ah,' she murmured, feeling as if a trap was closing around her.

'You must be patient,' Kahlil said, reading at least some of her thoughts. 'You must trust me.'

'Trust you?' Lucy repeated softly, flaring a wounded glance into his eyes. Had he forgotten what had happened between them on the first occasion they'd met? Had he forgotten how he'd left her—how he had disappeared out of her life without a trace?

'Of course,' he said impatiently, frowning a little.

'But I have airline tickets to take us home.'

'This is Edward's home,' Kahlil pointed out.

Once the official announcement was broadcast over the Abadanese airwaves the die would be cast, he reflected, watching Lucy closely. Then she would have to be far more open to any suggestions he made. His people would never countenance a child so close to the throne of Abadan leaving them to live in another country.

'*You* may leave whenever you wish,' he said smoothly.

Lucy stifled a gasp. Kahlil's meaning couldn't have been driven home with a sharper knife. She could go if she liked, but Edward would stay behind. She meant nothing to him, Lucy realised as she searched Kahlil's face. Having provided him with an heir, like one of his brood mares, she was now surplus to requirements.

What she saw was a cold, hard man. As far as Sheikh Kahlil ben Saeed Al-Sharif was concerned, with or without her, the path to claiming his son was clear. She had to get Edward away—she had to get them both away, as fast as she could.

'If you have pressing business to attend to back home,'

Kahlil continued levelly, as if they were discussing nothing more than that, 'you are of course free to leave Abadan the moment your contract here is completed.'

'With Edward?' Lucy tried one last time.

Kahlil remained silent.

'I will never leave Abadan without my son.'

'Then you will never leave Abadan.'

His words were like individual hammer blows, each one crushing her hope. But she had to stay strong—she had to stay strong for Edward.

'I'm sure we can find plenty to keep you happy here,' Kahlil observed.

Lucy was beyond speech, beyond argument. She could see Kahlil was growing restless as he laid out his master plan for her captivity. After all, she mused bitterly, it was only the small matter of her liberty and that of their son Edward under discussion—why should Sheikh Kahlil waste too much time over it?

And then Kahlil stood, and Lucy knew there was nothing left for either of them to say. The talking was over; only desperate action was left to her now.

'There may even be another contract for you,' he murmured pensively.

Still business! Did he think of nothing else? 'Don't trouble to invent work to keep me here, Kahlil. I don't need your charity.'

He made a light, surprised sound. 'I was talking about paid employment.'

Remembering a tender lover, as well as agonising over where that lover had gone, were no help to her now, Lucy told herself firmly. That man had vanished, leaving Sheikh Kahlil of Abadan in his place. And she would need money very soon if she was to escape. She had brought very little cash with her—not anticipating any of this. In this instance she couldn't afford to be proud.

'Perhaps an advance in cash on the work I have already completed?'

'In cash?'

'That would be great—'

'Where would you spend it? You can have everything you and Edward need charged to my account.'

Bought and paid for? Lucy thought angrily. No chance! But she clamped her mouth shut, determined not to say anything that would harm her cause. It was far better to let Kahlil think she was content with her lot, and with the arrangements he had made for her. She decided to ignore his personal offer to finance her, and keep to the safer option of what was properly owed to her.

'Perhaps part of what I'm owed could be paid into my account back home, and I could receive part in cash here,' she said casually, to deflect his suspicion. 'I would like to do some shopping—for Edward and for myself. It would be good for both of us to leave the confines of the palace, and I'd like to see the town.'

'Very well,' Kahlil agreed. 'That doesn't sound unreasonable.'

She must feel the palace was oppressive, Kahlil conceded, and if she did, chances were his son did too. The Golden Palace was his home; he loved it. But he could see that for Lucy it held quite different associations. It was time for him to show he could be merciful. He would ease the restrictions a little in order for her to see Edward's future home in a different light.

'There is a shopping mall in town, a short drive away. I could take you.'

Lucy's heart sank, and her throat was so dry she had to force out the words. 'I couldn't trouble you—'

'It would be no trouble,' Kahlil assured her. He thought at once of introducing Edward to the brash delights of the luxury mall: to ice cream sundaes and toy shops, and children's entertainers who were employed to keep youngsters happy during opening hours.

'No, really—a bodyguard would be fine,' Lucy said, hoping her acceptance of the security measures he'd had put in place would be enough to convince him.

Kahlil made a swift mental reality check. A trip into town for a member of the ruling family was no picnic. Ideally, he should give notice. Extra security would be needed for crowd control; barriers would need to be erected. There would be dignitaries he should meet, walkabouts to perform—none of which would be very much fun for Edward. 'Very well,' he agreed reluctantly. 'I will arrange for one of my personal bodyguards to accompany you. But first let me give you some money—'

'No!' Lucy exclaimed without thinking, seeing him reach for his wallet. 'Absolutely not.'

'You agreed to an advance on your wages,' Kahlil reminded her.

Who could tell how much money she might need? Lucy reflected grimly. And not for shopping. 'OK,' she said, 'an advance which I will pay back.' And she would, however long it took, and from wherever she eventually had to send the cheque.

'Well, I'm glad that's settled,' Kahlil said, moving towards the door. 'The shops are open until late in the evening. Be ready to leave in an hour.'

Oh, I will, Lucy told herself tensely.

Kahlil saw her to the door, as distanced from her now as if she was indeed an employee, Lucy thought, as she gave him the barest of acknowledgements before leaving— enough for politeness, enough to allay his suspicions. But once he had closed the door behind her and she was alone in the corridor her mind ran with the opportunity Kahlil had unwittingly handed to her. Now she had both the means and the opportunity to escape.

Fisting her hands in triumph, she exclaimed fiercely, 'Yes!'

Butter wouldn't melt in her mouth—or that was what everyone would think, Lucy concluded with relief as she caught sight of her face in one of the many palace mirrors. Dressed casually, plainly, so as not to attract attention, she was pushing Edward in his stroller down the long corridor leading to the grand entrance.

If the attending servants only knew what she had planned, but fortunately, their mind-reading skills were not as highly developed as those of their master, or they would have stopped her by now. Even so, her heart was thundering so loudly in her ears it muffled everything else. The thought of what she was about to do was terrifying.

Stealing a glance over her shoulder, she took in the crop-haired older man Kahlil had insisted must accompany her. He was a trusted member of the palace security team, and looked sharp. But that couldn't be helped. She would have to try and find a way to outfox him.

She had to get out of Abadan. It was her only hope. She had to negotiate with the ruling family from a position of strength. She had no alternative but to carry out her plan, regardless of the hurdles Kahlil put in her way.

As the bodyguard loaded the stroller into the back of a Range Rover Vogue, Lucy double-checked the fastenings on Edward's car seat, so that it would appear natural for her to just slip in beside him on the back seat. That way she could take careful note of every landmark they passed without drawing attention to herself.

Her passport was safely stowed away in her shoulder bag. Now all she needed was the opportunity to take over the four-wheel drive. Then she intended to make for the

Embassy and seek sanctuary there with Edward until a flight home was arranged for her.

There were still a few loose ends to tie up on her existing design contract at the palace, Lucy remembered, chewing her knuckles with anxiety, but that couldn't be helped. Edward's future happiness was at stake, and their liberty. Nothing mattered compared to that. She would shoulder whatever consequences arose from the breach of contract in a safer environment...repay any money, do whatever it took.

Trying to calm herself, Lucy remembered she was supposed to be watching the road signs as they drew closer to the centre of the town; she had already missed quite a few. Sidelining her other concerns, she made herself concentrate on the direction they were taking. She spotted the flag marking the Embassy and relaxed a little. It shouldn't be too hard to find again, even if it was dark by the time they left the shopping mall. There were plenty of road lights, and the town centre was clearly marked.

The shopping mall in Abadan was fantastic, and after an hour or so Lucy knew she had never spent money so freely. But beneath the fun of watching Edward clap his hands with delight was the worrying undercurrent of their impending flight. The professional bodyguard wouldn't leave their side for a moment, and right now she had no idea how she was going to get away.

On their way back to the car park she was ready to try anything. And a risky idea had occurred to her. The buggy was loaded with brightly coloured parcels that Edward had refused to relinquish. She should have insisted that he allow them to be taken away and delivered to the palace, but now his stubbornness, so like his father's, played right into her hands. There was enough shopping to keep the bodyguard busy loading the four-wheel drive for quite a few minutes. 'Shall we go back to the palace instead?' she said to him pleasantly, when he asked her if she would like to have a coffee before leaving. Clearly Kahlil had instructed him to make sure that her every whim was accommodated. And it would be, Lucy determined. But not in the way that Kahlil intended. If he thought he could tame her with a bit of therapeutic shopping, he was wrong.

'If you're ready,' her shadow said politely, as he offered to take some of the bags from her.

Don't try to make a break too soon, Lucy warned herself as she thanked the man for his assistance. Edward was still hanging on to a couple of packages, and she hooked the rest onto the handles of the stroller. Everything hinged on keeping her head.

Fortunately Edward was asleep by the time they reached the off-roader. Waiting until the bodyguard had opened the rear door for her to climb in, Lucy took Edward carefully from the stroller to avoid waking him, and fastened him securely into the baby seat.

'I'll fire up the air-conditioning,' the bodyguard offered, knowing the heat might be uncomfortable once they left the precincts of the shopping centre.

'Would you?' Lucy said, hardly able to believe her luck. She felt a moment's guilt, because the man was so helpful, but, remembering the bigger picture, she hardened her heart. Closing Edward's door, Lucy watched the man climb into the driver's seat and start the engine. When he climbed out again to load the remaining parcels she waited for her chance as he pushed the door to. 'Do you need any help?' she asked, moving a step closer.

'No, I'm doing fine,' he said. 'You get in—this won't take a minute.'

'Oh, no,' Lucy exclaimed. 'I've dropped something— over by the door. Look—can you see it?'

'No problem. I'll get it for you,' he offered, turning back.

Lucy was in the driver's seat the moment his back was

turned. The boot was still open, but that couldn't be helped. Slipping the engine into gear, she stamped her foot down on the accelerator, and with a squeal of rubber on tarmac they were on their way, lurching over the kerb and barely missing the bodyguard as he wheeled around, realising a beat too late that he had been duped.

Peering through the windscreen as the Range Rover careered out of the car park and joined the main road, she made an abrupt U-turn across the double carriageway, bumping over the grass verge before heading at speed towards the outskirts of town, where she had first spotted the diplomatic quarter.

She had bargained on reaching the Embassy before Kahlil's guards could give chase, and certainly long before the police closed the roads. But she would have to stop somewhere soon to close the boot, Lucy realised, glancing anxiously through the mirror. She was already drawing attention, driving at speed with the back of the vehicle wide open. People were hitting their horns and gesticulating to warn her.

She looked back anxiously at Edward, and saw with relief that he was sleeping. Missing all the fun! Except that this wasn't fun, Lucy thought, forced to brake hard when her flight was abruptly aborted by a traffic snarl-up. She fought to control the Range Rover on the busy freeway as it skidded sideways, and was thrown back when it finally slammed to a halt on the hard shoulder. Gasping for breath, she wheeled round to check on Edward. He was still sleeping. And she could secure the back now.

Taking her chances, Lucy climbed out and quickly closed it up, oblivious to the shouts and horns of other motorists blasting in her ears. Running to the driver's door, she swung herself inside and cut back into the traffic while she was still slamming the door shut. It took her a few moments to calm down again, by which time she realised she had missed the turning. And now it was dark, and headlights were coming at her constantly. It was totally disorientating—and Kahlil had to know what had happened by now. Time was running out!

'Damn!' Lucy exclaimed softly, swerving off the busy dual carriageway by the first exit that came along. If she could work her way back into town, perhaps she could pick up the right road again.

But where was she now? she wondered, gazing around. She didn't have a clue. There were no streetlights to help her. She looked to left and to right, trying to make a decision. She wanted to head back the way she had come, but by the time she had looped her way off the main road it was impossible to tell which direction she was going in, and because she was in a dip the city lights had completely disappeared.

Totally disorientated, she carried on driving round the roundabout, looking for road signs, looking for anything that might help her. But there was nothing. And two of the exits off the roundabout were blocked by roadworks. That narrowed her choice down to two minor roads, neither of which were lit, or even surfaced properly. She would have to choose one of them, Lucy realised, and trust that it led back into town, or at the very least back onto the dual carriageway.

What option did she have? Lucy wondered anxiously. She would have to stay on the back roads for now, and trust to her sense of direction.

CHAPTER EIGHT

Now she was on higher ground Lucy could see the lights of the city in the distance. If she kept them in front of her, she knew nothing could go wrong. But there were enormous potholes on the unmade road and she was making painfully slow progress. And then the clouds shifted, allowing the moon to light her way. She saw that the track had narrowed, and there were no turning places if anything came towards her.

After a wide, sweeping curve in the road, the dirt and gravel changed to sand, and a rock face blanked off the passenger window, blocking her view of the reassuring lights in the distance. Reversing back seemed the right thing to do, but when she stopped and looked out of her own window she saw a sheer drop outside the driver's door. She couldn't risk it. Not with Edward in the back. She had to press on. She slowed the vehicle to a crawl. Frequent checks showed she was going downhill, and the track was widening out again too. Surely it couldn't be much longer before she could turn around.

Kahlil's rage was like a whirlwind, sweeping all before it. His anger was the silent ferocious kind that kicked everyone's brain into gear in an instant. The helicopters were already scrambled; roadblocks were set up. He had taken no more than five minutes to change into desert gear and grab the equipment he might need, and then the Hummer was waiting for him in the courtyard, engine running, the bodyguard who had accompanied Lucy and Edward sitting in the passenger seat. He would debrief him once they got on the road.

He should flay him alive, Kahlil thought, leaping into the driver's seat and slamming the door before the servants could get to it, but he had to admit to a grudging admiration for the man. It had taken some courage to return to the palace without either one of his charges. And he was just as guilty of underestimating Lucy Benson himself, Kahlil reflected as he pulled out of the palace gates. He had underestimated her and made the mistake of trusting her.

'The tracking device is working, I take it?' he said, dipping his head to look up at the night sky to assess the weather.

All the royal vehicles were fitted with tracking devices— something he could only be grateful Lucy couldn't know about. As long as it was functioning, and the weather was kind, it would be easy to find her.

'It is functioning, Majesty,' the bodyguard confirmed, still professional and calm in spite of his blunder. 'But the weather reports are bad.'

'Then we shall just have to hope we get to them before the sand blows up,' Kahlil murmured, not liking what he was seeing out of the windscreen.

As they approached the shopping mall he said abruptly, 'Did you see which way they went?'

'She crossed the dual carriageway and headed towards the roundabout—'

'Where the roadworks are being carried out?' Kahlil demanded, and before the man could answer he added grimly, 'Two of the roads are closed. I only hope she isn't heading for the desert.'

Silence hung heavy between the two men as the implications sank in. The bodyguard began calling up his colleagues on the radio as Kahlil concentrated on driving, his glance flicking edgily from the road to the screen of the satellite system positioned in front of them. Inwardly, he was raging. She had dared to abscond from the palace with his son, the eventual heir to the throne of Abadan—no punishment was great enough for that.

But any thoughts of retribution would have to wait, Kahlil realised as he noticed the way the clouds were scudding across the moon. The imperative now was to find Lucy and Edward before it was too late.

'Which way?' he said, thinking out loud as he slammed to a halt at the roundabout.

'I'm sorry—'

'Sorry?' he said abruptly, turning to the man at his side. 'It's a bit late for that.'

'The news I have just received, Majesty,' the man explained, brandishing the receiver in his hand, 'Miss Benson *is* heading for the desert.'

Kahlil swore eloquently. 'Can we still track her?'

'For the moment. But a sandstorm is blowing up.'

'Which road did she take?'

'Towards the border.'

'Alert the border patrols. Have them converge on the vehicle. The helicopters will have to return to base because of the weather, but we can follow them by road.'

A wave of anxiety washed over Kahlil as the bodyguard busied himself with the radio again. A sandstorm could stop the vehicle dead in its tracks and cover it in minutes. The terrain, already short on landmarks, could be transformed beyond recognition in the same amount of time. Even the most sophisticated satellite communication would prove useless if the Range Rover and everyone in it was buried beneath metres of sand.

Every muscle in his body clenched tight at the thought. She didn't know it yet, but Lucy and Edward were in very real danger. The desert was merciless, even to those who

Get FREE BOOKS and a FREE GIFT when you play the...

LAS VEGAS
GAME

Just scratch off the gold box with a coin. Then check below to see the gifts you get!

YES! I have scratched off the gold box. Please send me my **2 FREE BOOKS** and **gift for which I qualify.** I understand that I am under no obligation to purchase any books as explained on the back of this card.

306 HDL D7Y6   106 HDL D7XW

FIRST NAME   LAST NAME

ADDRESS

APT.#   CITY

STATE/PROV.   ZIP/POSTAL CODE   (H-P-08/05)

7	7	7	Worth TWO FREE BOOKS plus a BONUS Mystery Gift!
🍒	🍒	🍒	Worth TWO FREE BOOKS!
🔔	🔔	☘	TRY AGAIN!

DETACH AND MAIL CARD TODAY!

BUSINESS REPLY MAIL

FIRST-CLASS MAIL   PERMIT NO. 717-003   BUFFALO, NY

POSTAGE WILL BE PAID BY ADDRESSEE

HARLEQUIN READER SERVICE

3010 WALDEN AVE

PO BOX 1867

BUFFALO NY 14240-9952

NO POSTAGE
NECESSARY
IF MAILED
IN THE
UNITED STATES

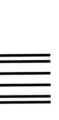

knew it intimately as he did. But to foreigners, a young woman with a child, probably with no water to sustain them through the heat of the day, and no blankets to warm them during the long desert night, it was nothing short of a disaster.

He guessed Lucy was already disorientated and frightened. He could only hope she had enough sense to find some high ground and park up before the forces of nature took over and hid the vehicle from sight—maybe for good.

The initial adrenalin rush that had accompanied Lucy's break for freedom had long since subsided. The weather had changed so rapidly, and with no warning whatsoever. One minute she had been driving along on a bright, clear night, with the moon as well as a good peppering of stars to light her way, and the next she was in a total blackout.

Remembering the precipice that had crept up on her earlier, she kept her speed as slow as possible. She had managed to turn the vehicle around, but she could not find the same track she had taken to come down into the valley. The city lights were gone, and the wind was growing stronger every minute. The Range Rover rocked alarmingly every time it was caught by one of the savage blasts, and sand covered the windscreen because the wipers had given up. And now she noticed there was very little fuel left in the tank. But at least they were on the move—they would surely encounter some form of civilisation soon…

As the steering wheel bucked in her hand Lucy let out a short scream, and when they juddered to a halt she realised they had a flat tyre. There was no way she could risk trying to change it on shifting sand, with the wind threatening to turn the vehicle over at any minute. Swinging round, she checked on Edward, and saw with relief that he was still sleeping. But they had no lights, no fuel, and her phone was dead too, she realised, flinging it aside with frustration. Now all she could do was switch off the engine and wait for the storm to subside.

Kahlil swore when the satellite screen went blank. 'Let's press on.'

'But where, Majesty? Which way?'

'We've chosen a trail; we'll stay on it. The road forked after its descent into the valley—she may not have noticed if she tried to turn around. We'll keep to the left, take our chances.' And just hope I've got it right, he thought grimly.

The wind was screaming as it whipped the sand into heavy curtains of dust and grit, and Kahlil knew that even he, with his encyclopaedic knowledge of the desert, might get it wrong.

'Did you get through to the border patrols before we lost the signal?'

When the man confirmed that he had, Kahlil acknowledged the information with a curt dip of his chin. But he didn't relax at all. Even using a pincer movement, this only gave them two slim chances to find one precious grain of sand in the desert.

It was like being in a riverbed in full flood, Lucy thought. She had never noticed how like water sand could be. The sand she knew was harmless, and inactive, but this sand, blowing before the wind, was deadly. It ran in gullies, filling every nook and cranny, and rose in waves to flood the larger indentations in the land.

She risked opening the window to lean out, and got a mouthful as well as her eyes full of sand for her trouble. And now it was already well over the wheel hubs, creeping rapidly up the sides of the vehicle. Even if she could have changed the flat tyre there was no way they were going anywhere now. But there were still rock formations, standing proud of the sand, and if the worst came to the worst, she would take Edward and escape through the back window. She would climb up as high as she could, and wait there for the wind to die down.

Slamming back in her seat, Lucy shut her eyes tight and forced back tears of sheer terror. How could she take a baby outside the vehicle in this? But what would happen to them both if she stayed where she was?

After a few minutes of bitter reflection, during which she blamed herself for everything, something around her changed. Holding her breath, she listened. It hardly seemed possible. She opened her eyes, and then opened the window and leaned out. As fast as it had blown up, the sandstorm was dying down again.

The moon was like a giant spotlight, pooling light around the vehicle as the clouds of dust subsided. But there was still no sign of a road. Even the rocks she had hoped to climb up to escape the river of sand had completely disappeared in the few minutes she had looked away from them. The land outside the vehicle was a moonscape, a featureless blank, Lucy saw, her relief swiftly turning to despair. How could anyone hope to find them now?

She started shivering with terror, and with cold too. But there were travel rugs in the back, as well as a bottle of water she had picked up in the shopping mall, along with some of Edward's favourite food. At least she had enough for a picnic when he woke up.

She hadn't known silence could be so absolute, Lucy realised as she tucked a rug around Edward. Backing out of the door, she stood very still, staring around in wonder. The sky was quite clear, and looked like a piece of black velvet studded with diamonds. But there were no city lights to offer any comfort, and no roads to help her get her bearings. There was no sign of habitation at all. And her phone still refused to work.

At least Edward was warm, and they had some provisions and water to keep them going. They would be found. She had to believe that.

Kahlil exclaimed viciously beneath his breath. The border patrols had reported picking up a weak signal from Lucy's vehicle, but it had died again. Slamming his fists down on the steering wheel with frustration, he threw the gears into reverse.

'She's obviously in a dip,' he said. 'We'll retrace our steps—this time down at the lowest point.'

'But Majesty,' the bodyguard protested, knowing his primary task was to protect the heir to the throne, and only after that his son, 'the surface will be treacherous.'

'All the more reason to hurry, then,' Kahlil told him curtly, swinging the wheel around. 'You concentrate on trying to restore the satellite link.'

'Yes, sire,' the man agreed reluctantly.

Lucy was wishing a different set of circumstances had brought her to the desert. It was so beautiful. She might have been alone on the planet with Edward. Stars like so many friendly eyes seemed to be keeping watch over them until rescue came.

Now she was going crazy, Lucy thought, pulling her rug a little tighter around her shoulders as she climbed into the back seat next to Edward. There was nothing at all romantic about their situation. The valley through which she had been driving had disappeared, and they had very nearly been buried alive. Clinging to Edward for comfort, she rested her face next to his and tried not to wake him with her shaking...

She had been dozing, Lucy realised, jerking awake. How long until dawn? She leaned over to peer out of the window. There was a faint lilac shadow above the horizon that filled her with hope. And then she noticed something else. At first she thought she was hallucinating, or maybe it was just wishful thinking. She checked to see that it wasn't moonlight refracting off the sand coating the glass. But the pinpricks of light didn't stay still. As she narrowed her eyes to try and make them out, they seemed to be dancing up and down. It was headlights! Coming their way! Vehicles being driven at such speed they were bouncing over the sand dunes. Any minute now they would be found!

Rescued! Lucy gave a sharp cry of relief, then as quickly as it had come, her elation died. It could be anyone—bandits or thieves—and she had no way of protecting Edward. She stared out again. The vehicles were closing in fast.

Quickly releasing the buckles on the baby seat, she hauled the half-sleeping child onto her knee. Wrapping him completely in the travel rug, she pushed open the door with her foot and went to climb out. But the trucks had already drawn up in formation around her. There was no escape, Lucy realised, shrinking back inside the Range Rover. And now she saw they were army vehicles. But whose army?

Her fear communicated itself silently to the warm little bundle on her knee. Edward might be small, but he was strong, and it took all her strength to stop him staring out of the window.

'Please—please don't,' she begged, drawing him down below the sill. In trying to protect him she had brought him into worse danger than ever, Lucy realised, covering his head with her arm as she cautiously looked out. Their doors were locked. She'd already checked that. But men were starting to exit the army trucks—men in uniform, with guns at their sides. They could easily shoot out the locks—or worse. And the moon was brighter than ever, acting like a searchlight for the soldiers.

There was not a chance that she could get out with Edward, and even if there was where would she go? Beyond the circle of moonlight the desert was completely black. She couldn't risk it, Lucy realised, clutching Edward to her as the soldiers formed a tight ring around them.

Their appearance was terrifying. Dressed all in black, with baggy trousers and tunics secured by broad leather belts holding a sheath for curving scimitars, just their glittering eyes showed beneath the black *howlis* they wore wound around their heads—and each pair of eyes was trained on her!

She heard one of the men issue instructions, in Arabic, and then he pointed away from the Range Rover. She turned to look through the back window to see what he was showing the other men. Racing up from the rear, another vehicle, headlights flashing, was approaching at speed.

And then everything seemed to happen at once. The leader of the men approached the side of the car where Lucy was crouching with Edward, hammered on the window and with imperative gestures demanded she get out.

Stricken with panic, and only aware of the gun at his side, she fumbled with the door handle, finally managing to free the catch. But as the door swung open, she shrank back, clutching Edward tight—too tight. With a yowl of protest he broke away, and before Lucy knew what was happening the man had leaned in and snatched him from her.

With a cry she launched herself after them. But, stumbling on the treacherous sandy ground, she made achingly slow progress as she chased after them in shoes meant for town. The wind was still gusting in spiteful little eddies, and she had sand everywhere—in her eyes, her mouth, and her ears. Finally the man stopped, and Edward was within her reach! But as she lunged forward to take him back someone stepped in her way.

'Kahlil!' Lucy sobbed.

'Allah be praised—you are safe!' he cried hoarsely, seizing Edward.

But Edward was fully awake now and did not recognise

the man in front of him—the fearsome figure with a black *howlis* wrapped around his head and only his glittering eyes on show. 'Mumma!' he screamed in panic, reaching for Lucy.

For a moment Lucy hung back, certain that prison or worse was to be her fate. Kahlil had not even acknowledged her presence.

He turned and looked down at her, his eyes black and hard. 'You had better hold your son,' he said coldly, 'and then follow me.'

CHAPTER NINE

LUCY had never seen such contained fury. It was all the more alarming because Kahlil didn't need to raise his voice to have the most hardened desert soldiers back away as he strode through them. He opened the door of his vehicle and helped her to climb in. Lucy seized some comfort where she could, in the warmth of Edward's chubby arms pinned around her neck, and the texture and touch of his soft face pressed hard against her own.

She sat in silence, holding Edward, waiting for Kahlil, who was issuing orders to his men. One by one the trucks turned away, heading towards the silvery light threading across the horizon. Then, whirling on his heels, Kahlil strode back, swung in to the driver's seat and slammed the door shut.

'There is no baby seat,' he said, without sparing her a glance. 'I have never had need for one. I take it you can keep my son safe on your knee during the journey?'

'I see no reason why not,' Lucy said quietly. 'I have kept him safe this far—without your assistance or anyone else's.'

They drove in tense silence for quite a while. Lucy had no idea where they were heading, and didn't much care, as long as when they arrived she could keep Edward with her. Glancing across at Kahlil, she saw that his anger had not lessened at all.

'Do you know what you've done?' he said, taking his cue from her glance. 'You could have been killed—and Edward too! What were you thinking of?'

'I had to get away. I couldn't stay locked up with my son like a prisoner in the Golden Palace.'

'He's my son too—'

'Yes, he's our son,' Lucy said. 'But, more than that, Edward is his own person. We should both respect that.'

'Don't you dare talk to me about respect,' Kahlil warned tensely, 'when you've shown me none.' Ripping off his desert headdress, he tossed it angrily behind his seat. And, seeing him properly for the first time, Edward exclaimed with pleasure and reached out.

Kahlil's face softened immediately, and without taking his attention from the road he took Edward's hand in a gentle grasp and brought it to his lips. 'Quite an adventure, little man,' he murmured. 'Where the hell were you going with him?' he said under his breath, shooting a glance at Lucy. 'What on earth did you think you were doing, heading out into the desert without proper supplies, in the middle of the night?'

'It was early evening when we set off, and I had no intention of going into the desert. A road was closed. I became disorientated—' Lucy stopped. Why should she have to defend herself? Suddenly she felt very tired. She couldn't summon the spirit to engage in the type of debate Kahlil was after on the rights and wrongs of the situation. All she was concerned with now was that Edward was no longer in danger. She wanted nothing more than to hold him, let go of the fear in her mind for a few hours, and sleep.

'You might never have been found.'

Kahlil's voice jerked her back to full attention again,

'I should have realised you could not be trusted.'

'That's a terrible thing to say. Hurt me if you must, but remember that it was you who put me in a position where I felt like a prisoner—where I thought you were going to take Edward...' It was no good, Lucy realised, seeing Kahlil's face was unresponsive, still hardened against her.

'If it had been left up to you I would never have known Edward existed,' he said coldly.

'How dare you judge me?' Lucy exclaimed. 'You were the one who slept with me and then left like a thief in the night. You didn't even have the decency to reveal your true identity, let alone leave your telephone number.'

Kahlil controlled his desire to snap back. He knew what Lucy said about that night was true. And he could not remain immune to how desperately low and weary she was. It brought home to him how terrified she must have been. Yes, she had been foolish, and reckless, and had set herself against him, but it gave him no pleasure to browbeat her more when she was so clearly at her lowest ebb.

His emotions were in turmoil, Kahlil realised tensely. He was relieved she was safe, but angry that he cared. She had stolen his son from him in every way that a woman could steal a child away. If he were only in his right mind he would never be able to forgive her. Seeing the state she was in, and the even sorrier state to which his angry words had reduced her, gave him no satisfaction. But he should throw every reprimand he could at her. She had put herself as well as the child in mortal danger. She must learn to respect the desert as he did.

Glancing across, he saw Lucy was swaying in her seat. She was ashen-faced, totally spent. The most basic human instinct he possessed demanded he take care of her. 'There's water and food in the back—just reach across,' he said curtly.

'Thank you,' she murmured. And he couldn't help noticing how she saw to Edward's needs before her own, or how her hands trembled as she struggled with the water container.

'Where are you taking us?' Lucy said, feeling a little more composed once she had nibbled the fruit and cheese Kahlil insisted she eat. The moon had slipped behind a cloud again, and without fixed points of reference she couldn't imagine how he knew where he was going.

'We're going to my hunting lodge,' he said. 'It's closer than the palace.'

Lucy was relieved they were speaking again, but she was still badly shaken after the ordeal, and Kahlil's cold manner left her in no doubt as to his feelings on her flight from the palace. 'Will it take long?' she said, keen to keep the tenuous line of communication between them open.

'It won't take long now we are out of the *wadi*—the dried-up riverbed,' he explained. 'All the loose sand collects there and has been slowing our progress.'

'I see.'

'We will be quiet now. My son must sleep.'

His son! Kahlil made her feel like a stranger, an onlooker in Edward's life, whereas he was the one who had stepped in to make things right. But she had no one to blame but herself. As far as Kahlil was concerned, with her flight from the palace she had forfeited the right to care for Edward. And in Abadan Kahlil's word was law. Like his father's. The chance of taking Edward out of the country now, Lucy accepted grimly, was absolutely nil.

She didn't realise that she had fallen into an exhausted slumber until she woke when the vehicle slowed to a crawl. Instantly awake, she looked around. Her first sight of Khalil's hunting lodge came as a complete shock. She had been expecting something along the lines of the Golden Palace, something towering and vast, monumentally impressive. But in a blinding flash of understanding she knew that the Golden Palace was a show, and what she was looking at now reflected the other, and perhaps the true side of Kahlil's family coin.

Nothing must have changed in a thousand years—two thousand years, Lucy guessed, gazing around in wonder. The sky, like an arc over their heads, was silver-grey and pink, with dashes of tangerine where the sun was just starting to creep over the horizon. But dozens of torches still burned brightly around the encampment, illuminating tented pavilions grouped around a limpid oasis. It was a magical scene, like something she might have dreamed of. But there was a feeling of impermanence about it, as if like all the other desert landmarks the camp might shift and change, and even disappear entirely within the space of a few short minutes.

When Edward murmured in his sleep Lucy turned her attention to him, dropping a kiss on his smooth brow, feeling a rush of relief that he was safe. It had been a very long night for them both, she reflected sleepily.

Kahlil brought the vehicle to a halt outside one of the grand tents. There was a guard in Arab dress waiting for them, accompanied by two women. They all bowed low as Kahlil swung out of the driver's seat.

And then the guard was at Lucy's side of the vehicle, reaching in and lifting Edward out before she realised what was happening. She barely had time to voice a protest, and was forced to watch as Kahlil received his sleeping child into his arms and kissed his face.

Closing his eyes for a moment, Kahlil raised his face to the sky in thankfulness, and at that moment Edward woke. Instead of bursting into tears, as Lucy had fully expected, he smiled up at Kahlil with complete confidence. And then he even tried to grab hold of the guard's beard as his father took him away.

A stab of anguish pierced Lucy's heart as she hurried after them. She could see how happy father and son were to be reunited. And Kahlil was so tender with Edward she couldn't help but feel threatened. To her surprise, Kahlil stopped and, waving the servants away, waited for her to catch up.

'Just a word,' he said, dipping his head to speak to her discreetly. 'We have a chance here to discuss all the implications of our situation before it becomes general knowledge.'

'*It* is called Edward,' Lucy said, bridling at the authoritative tone. 'And do we always have to argue like this in front of him?'

'Maybe if things had been different—'

'Maybe if you'd allowed them to be, Kahlil—or is it Kahl?' Lucy shot back angrily.

'Do you think I've forgotten?' Kahlil asked her in a low, impassioned voice. 'And do you think I've forgotten a single detail I've learned about Edward since I discovered he was my son?'

'He's my son too!' Lucy retorted in a furious whisper. 'He doesn't even know you!'

'Haven't you done enough damage? Kahlil demanded, catching hold of Lucy's arm to bring her alongside him as he took off towards the entrance of the nearest pavilion. 'Don't try and put me in the wrong, Lucy. It was you who put Edward's life in danger with this foolhardy expedition— and you who tried to deny me my son!'

His staccato accusations rained down on her like bullets. Lucy accepted that everything Kahlil said was true, but there would have been no need for subterfuge had he remained with her long enough for them to exchange personal details twenty-one months ago. And no need for her flight from the palace if she had not been isolated there with an imagination that filled in every blank with dread.

They were both to blame. But all that mattered now, Lucy realised, gazing at their son, who was watching them both intently, was that Edward was safe. She smiled at him reassuringly, and Edward smiled back. But as Kahlil led them into the pavilion it was his shoulder into which Edward nestled his head.

Setting Edward down on a bank of cushions, Kahlil lowered the heavy curtain across the entrance to keep out the wind and sand. As he turned up the flame on an old oil lamp Lucy noticed the brazier glowing brightly in one corner. The tent was really cosy, she realised with surprise. The chill of the desert night seemed far away here. But still the modern world intruded, when Kahlil spoke into his mobile phone.

Once again his expression was hard and fierce. She guessed the call was to confirm the stand-down of his troops now that she had been found. But when the call ended and he turned to look at Edward she saw his face change completely. Now he was warm, and wry, and full of humour, and he made Edward laugh. Then he glanced her way and he changed again; his eyes were cold and steady, as if he was warning her to expect nothing from him in the way of forgiveness.

Kahlil would fight for his son. Lucy was more certain of that than ever. And when Edward was old enough to understand he would fight for the right to see his father. She was on the outside already, just where Kahlil wanted her.

The same guard who had greeted them on arrival slipped through the curtain and made a swift bow of obeisance to Kahlil. The two men smiled, and even Lucy smiled when she saw Edward reaching up as if he wanted to tug the soldier's beard again. She didn't need to know the language to hear the pride in Kahlil's voice. She guessed the guard must have praised Edward's courage, and she was proud of her son too, but ice trickled through her veins as she watched him interacting with his father. It seemed to her that Edward was already part of another world...

'I am sending Edward to sleep in one of the women's tents,' Kahlil said, turning to her at last, 'so that he can get some rest. They will see to him,' he insisted, when Lucy began to protest. 'And you can see him as soon as he wakes up. We will bathe now, and then we will talk.'

Kahlil had assumed control of the whole situation—of her

life, Lucy realised. Normally she would have stood her ground, but right now she was exhausted, both mentally and physically. And how could she subject Edward to any more conflict between his parents?

'The minute he wakes up, they'll call me?' she said, looking for reassurance in that staggeringly handsome face made of stone.

'They'll call you,' Kahlil said.

There was already a new slant to Edward's life, Lucy realised as he went willingly with the guard. Sitting confidently on the man's shoulders, he gave her a wave, and she gave him a wave back, and a smile. But she couldn't help feeling Kahlil had set a new regime in place for Edward: one that was harsh and demanding, perfectly suited to a fledgling desert prince.

She flared a look of anguish at Kahlil. How could he know anything about Edward's needs? Their son was still a baby.

'What's that in Edward's hand?' she said, stepping forward with alarm just as the heavy curtain was about to fall back into place.

'My gauntlet,' Kahlil said without concern.

'Of course—you hunt with falcons,' she murmured, realising Edward must have found it amongst the cushions.

And when he was old enough Sheikh Kahlil ben Saeed Al-Sharif would give his son a hawk, and teach him to ride bareback, and to shoot straight, like a true Abadanese—all the things she could never hope to teach him.

How could she deny Edward the other half of his heritage? Taking him from Abadan would deny him his birthright. When he grew up he would blame her for the loss. And when that happened she would lose him for ever. She had to search for a compromise. It had to be possible. Yes, Kahlil could teach Edward how to be a leader of men, but she could teach him how to care.

'Your bath has been run for you,' Kahlil said, gesturing carelessly to another opening in the pavilion Lucy gathered must lead to a second room. 'I will return shortly, and then we will talk.'

Lucy resisted the impulse to salute. If the situation hadn't been so serious she might have done. She was dead on her feet, but thankfully she hadn't lost her sense of humour, she reflected ruefully. And that had saved many a captive before her. She turned at a discreet cough to see two serving women smiling as they beckoned to her from the entrance to the second room.

Was she to be prepared for the Sheikh? Lucy wondered cynically as she viewed the deep bath. The surface was completely covered with rose petals, and the scent was sublime. But the women were still waiting for her to make some response, and showed no sign of leaving her as they stood smiling with stacks of fluffy white towels balanced on their outstretched arms.

Lucy bowed and smiled, and managed a few words of Abadanese which she could see were appreciated. She was delighted at the prospect of washing off all the sand and grit she had collected during the long night, but she had no intention of bathing with an audience. Taking some towels, she thanked them again and then walked to the entrance and stood beside it, so that there could be no misunderstanding. Exchanging swift glances, they pointed to a robe in ice-blue silk and then, bowing their way out, they left.

It was a relief to know she wouldn't have to wear her grimy clothes any more, and this was ecstasy…bliss, Lucy thought, sinking a little deeper into the warm, fragrant water. And it was all the better for being so unexpected in the middle of the desert. A bath made for two—that thankfully she was enjoying by herself.

Her thoughts turned immediately to Kahlil. He had come to rescue the heir of Abadan; she knew that. But it was hard to shut out the image of his strong hands controlling the wheel as she sat next to him. And then it was a very small step to recall how those hands had also controlled her, bringing her pleasure beyond anything she could ever have imagined… But Lucy knew that was one thought-robbing indulgence she could not afford.

She sat up so abruptly the water crashed over the edge of the bath. She had a crisis on her hands; this was not the time to be diverted by fantasies that belonged to the past.

'Are you still in there?'

She tensed at the sound of Kahlil's voice, realising she was aroused, and that now she was feeling guilt and shock in equal measure. 'Just a minute,' she called out, 'I'll be right there.'

Water splashed everywhere as Lucy leapt out of the bath and grabbed the towels. She wrapped herself in them quickly, as if at any minute Kahlil might come striding in and find her pink and flushed naked body stirred by thoughts of him.

Drying herself quickly, she towelled her wet hair as best she could and contained it in a towel turban on top of her head. The silk robe felt wonderful next to her skin—but she would have to do without underwear, she realised, frowning. It couldn't be helped. Kahlil was waiting, and she wanted to get their discussion over with as quickly as possible. Bracing herself, she went out to face him.

For a moment they stared at each other from either end of the tented pavilion. Kahlil had changed too, into a black silk robe that hinted provocatively at the magnificent form beneath. His head was uncovered, his thick black hair was still damp from bathing, and there was a slight flush to his high cheekbones, as if his bath had taken the form of a rigorous workout in the limpid oasis.

Lucy felt her body respond to him, melting beneath his stare. It was as if his black glittering gaze had the power to undress her—not that it took much imagination to see her nipples erect beneath the gossamer fabric. Instinctively she raised her arms to cover her chest.

'Don't,' he murmured, continuing to stare at her.

'We have to talk,' Lucy said huskily. 'And I want to go to Edward.'

'He is being well cared for,' Kahlil assured her. 'He was still awake when I left him.'

The same flood of frustration, of resentment at Kahlil's interference must have shown clearly on her face.

'He at least enjoyed the adventure,' Kahlil said soothingly, holding out his hand to her.

Lucy stared at him like a fool. Was she supposed to take his hand now, as if they were lovers, and allow him to take her wherever he chose?

'Don't you want to see him?'

'Of course I do,' Lucy exclaimed, coming to with a start. Her bare feet made no sound as she padded rapidly across priceless rugs, hurrying towards the curtained entrance.

'Wait,' Kahlil said as she drew level with him. 'You will need to cover yourself first, and put on some sandals.'

He slipped a cotton robe over her head himself and, removing the towelling turban, replaced it with a beautifully jewelled scarf in a deeper shade of blue.

'To keep out the sand now your hair is clean again,' he murmured, anticipating her refusal. 'And now these,' he said, dipping down to retrieve a pair of simple sandals that had been left for her—nothing more than a strip of leather to fit between her toes on a cork sole. 'Now you are dressed for the desert,' he said with approval.

And this time he stood aside to let her pass, Lucy noticed with interest. When all she had anticipated was his anger he showed respect. Kahlil was really a very confusing and complex man. But as he showed her into another vast tent Lucy remembered Kahlil's heritage was part Eastern, part

Western—the perfect mix in a man, maybe, but dangerous for her, when everything hinged on keeping her wits about her for the sake of Edward's safe return home.

'Safia will take care of Edward for you,' Kahlil said. 'She speaks very good English.'

Jolted from her reverie, Lucy smiled at the older woman. Edward had fallen asleep at last, clearly exhausted by his adventures. And as she gazed down at his pink cheeks she was relieved that her worries about him had been removed for now.

'You must be exhausted too,' Kahlil observed, standing at the other side of the cot. 'Would you rather sleep before we talk?'

'I couldn't sleep,' Lucy said honestly.

'Then why don't we leave Safia and Edward here?' he suggested. 'My tent is close by.'

'Yes,' she said.

Lucy knew she wouldn't be able to rest until she had found out how Kahlil intended to proceed. Once she knew that she could decide upon her own actions. But she felt a little reassured. Kahlil seemed more reasonable here. The desert seemed to have a soothing effect on him. Maybe now they could have a balanced discussion about Edward's future…

'When the sun rises,' Kahlil murmured, pausing beside the crib to gaze down at his sleeping son, 'you will see the mountains that mark the borders of your kingdom from this window.'

Lucy felt as if she had been slapped in the face—brought round from her romantic daydreams with a blow. She had been such a fool to think Kahlil would soften. He was just as tyrannical, just as hard and uncaring as he had ever been. She had mistaken his confidence in the outcome of their discussions for compromise, his easy manner for forgiveness. But as far as Sheikh Kahlil ben Saeed Al-Sharif was concerned his son's future was already cast in stone.

CHAPTER TEN

KAHLIL had tea brought to them in his luxurious quarters. Hot and sweet for her shock, Lucy gathered, as the liquid burned her tongue.

'Patience,' Kahlil counselled, removing the small vase-like glass container from her hands. They were shaking, Lucy noticed as he poured some iced water for her from a gold pitcher studded with jewels.

'May I suggest we move outside to watch the sun rising?' Kahlil suggested when she had drained her glass.

He was behaving so pleasantly, Lucy registered dimly, but she had to be cautious. She knew her normal wariness was cancelled out by exhaustion and shock. She followed him outside like an automaton, not sure she had the strength to battle with him, only knowing that with Edward's future at stake she would.

'I do this every time I come here,' Kahlil said, turning to Lucy and leading her forward out onto the veranda of his pavilion, where a bank of silk cushions had been set for them.

Lucy breathed with astonishment as she took in everything properly for the first time. The desert was laid out before them like a gently undulating beach. It stretched away to the jagged black mountain peaks Kahlil had spoken of to Edward. The play of light on rock and sand was extraordinary. The mountains in the far distance were still shrouded in mist against the silver-pink sky, but their snowy peaks were just visible. And as they watched the fiery fingers of desert sun reaching above the horizon the mist peeled back, revealing the massive range in all its splendour.

Lucy turned to look at Kahlil, gazing out across his desert kingdom. How tall and proud he was. His black robe, caught by the wind, moulded his limbs and outlined his magnificent physique. She longed to reach him—she could only hope that maybe he would make an effort too.

'I can see why you love it so much,' she said impulsively.

Did she really understand? Kahlil wondered as he turned to look at Lucy. Could she grow to love this land as he did? He stopped himself. That was an irrelevance. Then he saw her shiver again, and, finishing the tea he had been nursing in a single gulp, he went back inside the pavilion to find something warm for her.

Lucy started as Kahlil bent over her to wrap a silky-soft hand-woven blanket around her shoulders.

'You must be exhausted to still be shivering,' he said, arranging it deftly. 'It's really quite warm now.'

His touch was electrifying. He barely brushed her with his hands, but that had no relation to the intensity of her response. 'I am a little tired,' Lucy said to explain her reaction

'Blue is definitely your shade,' he added, straightening up, 'and I like the veil...very feminine.'

Tired as she was, Lucy lowered it from her head immediately, and flung it defiantly around her shoulders like a scarf.

Her hair was dry, and shimmered around her face like a golden nimbus, and he loved to see the challenge back in her eyes. Beautiful, Kahlil mused. Too bad there were so many complications... But he would have her, whatever difficulties would have to be overcome.

Lucy coloured as Kahlil looked at her. She knew she must keep the lines of communication open between them somehow. Outright defiance was no help to her cause. She had to use subtlety, and appear more malleable. 'These colours are lovely,' she said, admiring the lovely shawl he had

brought her. And the almost weightless wrap was quite use-
ful—to hide the evidence of her arousal, so intense, still so
easily provoked by Kahlil.

'Do you mind if I join you?' he said, glancing down at
the cushions where she was sitting.

Sheikh Kahlil asking permission for anything had to be a
first, Lucy thought with surprise. And how could she object?
It was his pavilion, his cushions, his desert kingdom. 'Of
course I don't mind.'

This was not what she had expected, Lucy realised as
Kahlil settled beside her. She was beginning to think her act
was unnecessary, he seemed so reasonable. Recriminations,
blame, anger, she had been prepared for. But this sudden
ease between them made her hope they could talk, settle
things amicably.

Confidence heightened her awareness of Kahlil's powerful body reclining so near to her own. She hadn't anticipated
sitting so close to him, but she could have predicted her
reaction. She was on fire. It was as if Kahlil had simply
stepped across all the divisions between them to bathe her
in desire.

They sat in silence, and very gradually Lucy became
aware that her muscles were unknotting. Deep down she
knew she should be tense, and alert, on her guard, but she
was not. She should be demanding answers, looking for
strategies to curb Kahlil's will, but she couldn't—not yet,
anyway. Just for a little while she wanted to believe that
everything would be all right. She wanted the beauty of the
desert to wash over them, to let the peace of their surroundings heal the rift between them. All right, Lucy reflected
dreamily, so it might be wishful thinking, but right now,
reclining on silk cushions so close to Kahlil, anything
seemed possible…

'Wake up…wake up, Lucy.'

Reluctantly, Lucy opened her eyes. And then she leapt

into an upright sitting position. She had been asleep in Kahlil's arms, resting her head on his shoulder! Her flesh still burned with the touch of him—she raised her hand in astonishment to her mouth. Was it a dream? She was sure she could feel the ghost of a kiss on her parted lips.

'What time is it?' she said, surfacing fast from her drowsy state.

'Almost lunchtime,' Kahlil said. 'I didn't want to wake you.'

But he had removed the wrap from her shoulders, and, looking up, Lucy saw that an awning had been erected over their heads to keep them in the shade. Even so it was hot. 'We haven't talked yet,' she said, fanning herself. All the good done by her sleep vanished as she remembered the events that had brought them to this point.

'Not yet,' Kahlil agreed, flexing his limbs and springing up. 'It will have to wait now. Edward will be ready to eat—'

'Edward! Where is he?'

'Where we left him,' Kahlil said, looking down at her, his expression hidden in the shadow cast by the giant canopy.

Lucy relaxed. 'Of course. I don't know what I was thinking.'

'He is well looked after, I can assure you. Your clothes will have been laundered if you would like to change back into them before lunch.'

Yes, she would like to change into something more conventional, Lucy thought, realising she was still wearing the exotic but rather impractical gowns. And as for lunch— Kahlil made it sound so civilised, so normal, but nothing about the situation was normal.

'I thought we would have lunch with our son—unless you prefer not to?'

And be excluded totally? 'Of course I'd like to.'

'Good. Edward will like that.'

The ribbon of fear that had started threading its way through Lucy's optimism drew tight. Kahlil sounded so confident, so sure. It was as if he had known Edward all his life and she was the outsider.

'I want to see him now,' she insisted, her throat tightening with apprehension. 'Before lunch, before I change—' She stopped, seeing the expression in Kahlil's eyes harden.

'Did you think I would have him stolen away while you were sleeping?'

Lucy reddened, knowing she had attempted to pull off something very similar.

'Don't worry, Lucy,' Kahlil said, reading her like a book. 'I don't work that way. Whatever action I take regarding my son will be out in the open, for all men to see, all men to judge.'

The thought of Kahlil taking action against her with all the might of Abadan's legal system behind him filled Lucy with dread. And then, gripping her arms, Kahlil looked deep into her eyes so she could not mistake the purpose in his.

'You don't know me at all, do you? Edward is fine. Safia is looking after him, as I told you she would. And when you are ready to go for lunch you will see him for yourself.'

It was subtle, but still there; Kahlil was dictating when she could and could not see Edward.

Her stomach contracted with resentment and with fear. Her escape attempt had failed utterly, and in fact she had only made things worse.

Lucy's swift intake of breath as emotion overtook her drew Kahlil to her. She was so strong, and to see her brought low, and to know that he was the cause of her distress, aroused feelings in him that were new. He didn't intend to kiss her. It was the last thing on his mind. He didn't mean to frighten her either, or to threaten her, and what he saw in her eyes was fear. It made him recognise his wish to bring her under his protection.

Lucy Benson was like a madness that possessed him, Kahlil realised as he drew her close. He wanted his son more than anything in the world, but he wanted Lucy as well. One the laws of Abadan would secure for him, the other he might have to seduce into submission. But he would have them both.

Even now, even at her lowest ebb, she fought him off. But as he drank in her sweetness, and murmured soft words in his own language to soothe her, she grew calmer, until at last she melted against him and slowly turned her face up for his kiss.

Kahlil's hunger surged when he saw the desire in Lucy's eyes. He ached with the need to pleasure her, to comfort and protect her. He wanted her in his bed, awaiting the pleasure he would bring her night after night...until he tired of her.

He had been forced to amend his plan to make her his mistress. The Constitution of Abadan required Edward to be a legitimate heir: for that he would have to marry Edward's mother.

It wasn't a problem, Kahlil reflected, seeing how Lucy hungered for him. She would agree to anything he suggested. Better still, she was a successful career woman. She would see the sense in putting a time limit on their arrangement. She would be hugely flattered that he wished to elevate her above the rank of mere mistress. She had everything to gain: money, prestige, the throne of Abadan for her son, for goodness' sake. What more could any woman want? And, although marriage with a woman like Lucy Benson would normally be unthinkable, it was expedient in this case, and would certainly legitimise their son as the law required.

And love?

Kahlil made a sound of derision deep in his throat as the crazy notion struck him out of nowhere. The lure of a throne, a fortune and a title would be more than enough for Lucy. He had seen the lie lived out in many other royal households. The stamp of royalty was all it took to convince even the most cynical of women that she was in love.

But now Lucy responded to his wordless growl with a soft, deep-seated whimper of her own, and Kahlil frowned, drawing back for a moment. In that instant she had seemed too trusting, too defenceless—

Love?

This time he dismissed the notion out of hand and kissed her again, passionately, hard, relishing the way she melted against him. *Lust is not love,* he scolded his inner voice triumphantly. *And lust is something I know all about.*

But as he deepened the kiss Kahlil wanted love on every level. He was hungry for it, starving. The erotic level was what he craved most now. He needed to lose himself in the silky darkness of her body, put thinking aside. He couldn't wait to tutor her in all the seductive mysteries of the East— a day of passion to seal their bargain.

'Lunch,' Lucy told him softly when he let her go.

'A late lunch,' he growled, swinging her into his arms.

'But Edward—'

'Is being taken care of,' he reminded her, dropping a quick, reassuring kiss on her brow as he carried her across the room.

It had been so long, too long, and the sexual attraction between them was explosive, their appetites insatiable. But both were aware of the clock ticking, and the promise they had made to share one meal together as a family for their son's sake.

Lucy cried out in ecstasy as Kahlil swung her round. In one move he was inside her, before they had made it to the bed. Her silk and cotton gowns were roughly pushed up out of the way so she could wrap her legs around his waist and urge him on. She was barely aware of anything now, other than Kahlil's full and total possession of her body, and her own overpowering need to find release.

Still pleasuring her, still sinking deep within her, Kahlil managed to shrug off his robe and mount the steps leading to the raised platform where they would lie together. Lucy lay heavily against his shoulder as he worked inside her, her mouth slack, her eyes glazed from a pure overdose of pleasure, and then she groaned as he lowered her down onto the very edge of the mattress. She was already tilted at an inviting angle, and uttered a small cry of alarm when he brought both her legs over his shoulders to open her wider still.

'I would never hurt you. If you want me to stop—'

'No!' she exclaimed fiercely.

Did he think her brazen? The thought slipped in and out of Lucy's mind like a shadow. But Kahlil knew her, he understood her needs... She let out a long, shuddering gasp as he began to tease her with shallow probes. She was reduced to crying out, to begging him for release with words she could hardly believe she knew. And then he went deeper still, until he was groaning with pleasure as much as she was as they hovered in intensely pleasurable suspension over the edge of the abyss.

They both wanted the moment to last for ever, and both knew equally that it could not. Lucy struggled hard to make the exquisite feeling last, to hold back, to stop herself falling, to hold on to the blissful moments. But Kahlil refused her this last indulgence and thrust into her rhythmically, moving slowly at first, and then deeper than she had ever known or thought possible. When he picked up the pace she was finally defeated, and gave a long wail of ecstasy as she tumbled into an endless dark tunnel of pulsing sensation.

'And now lunch,' he murmured when she had quietened.

'Lunch?' she said groggily.

'Take a shower,' Kahlil said. 'My bathroom is at your disposal.'

His words now were cold, so matter-of-fact it was as if another person entirely was speaking to her. Suddenly Lucy became aware that her clothes were bunched around her neck.

'Don't you want a shower?' she said, finding her voice dry and hoarse as she hurried to straighten them. But Kahlil was already halfway across the room.

'I have another bathroom through here,' he said, turning briefly to stare at her.

Of course, Lucy thought, falling silent. She might have known Sheikh Kahlil would be prepared for every eventuality, even out here in the desert.

'And don't take too long,' he said. 'We have another appointment, if you remember?'

Remember? As if she could forget their planned lunch with Edward! Lucy made a sharp, incredulous sound, but Kahlil had already gone.

News that their Prince had arrived had spread like wildfire amongst the tribesmen of the desert, and the chance to discuss Edward's future over a quiet family lunch was an impossible dream, Lucy realised as she emerged from the women's pavilion and saw the crowds. The event she had imagined would be private had been transformed into a ceremonial occasion. Though, as such, it surely had to be one of the most spectacular of its kind. She could hardly believe how many people had assembled in the hope of seeing Kahlil.

The cruel heat of midday had eased considerably by the time Lucy carried Edward up the wooden steps to the canopied area outside the royal pavilion. The light had taken on a mellow honey colour that seemed to bring out the occasional splash of bright colour, so that what she saw in front of her resembled a scene from a film. Lucy looked around in wonder. At the silken cushions heaped where she would sit. Overhead, a richly tented ceiling of white and gold silk cast a shade over the eating area below, and there were two side walls of silk undulating lazily in the breeze. The front of the pavilion was open to the elements and to the vast sandy expanse of desert, where all the nomadic people of Abadan had gathered.

There was an incongruous mix of old and new, Lucy noticed: something she was becoming accustomed to in Abadan. The decking beneath her feet would have been just as happy in a suburban garden back home, but this decking was covered with fabulous antique rugs that sank like dense pads of velvet beneath her sandalled feet.

Safia, who had accompanied her, had thought to bring some toys for Edward, but all he wanted to play with was his father's gauntlet.

There was still no sign of Kahlil, though Lucy guessed he would be amongst his people somewhere. Searching the crowds, she was surprised to see how many trucks were parked up alongside the camels at the edge of the assembly area.

'Roads criss-cross the desert now,' Safia informed her when she saw Lucy's puzzled glance light on the car park. 'Fuel is more readily available here in Abadan than water.'

'Of course,' Lucy said, realising this must be so in an oil-rich state. With a smile at Safia, she turned, shading her eyes, and stared out across the mass of people, still searching for Kahlil. And then she saw him—in the thick of it, a head taller than all the other men. He was examining some stallions that had been brought for his approval.

As if sensing her interest, he turned to look at her, and Lucy's heart leapt as their eyes locked. Whatever he might think of her, she had never felt more proud of Kahlil in that moment, or more pleased to think he was the father of her son. He looked every bit the Prince of Abadan, but there was tenderness in his face as his gaze dropped to Edward, playing happily at her side. Then he turned back to talk to the tribesmen again, completely absorbed in whatever it was they were saying to him.

Kahlil's sincerity shone through when he was speaking to them, Lucy realised with a pang of envy. The way banter passed easily between the men and their Prince showed how much they respected each other. This was what she wanted for Edward. She wanted him to grow up respecting others, and, in turn, to earn the right to have them respect him.

Kahlil had to do a double take when he noticed Lucy had arrived. And then he had to remind himself that duty took precedence over his personal life. Or had done up to now, he thought, as his astonished gaze swept over her again. Her resemblance to the photographs in his family archive had never struck him before, but it was quite incredible. He took in her casual attire, and the way she had swept up her long blonde hair into a no-nonsense ponytail, and didn't have to move a step closer to know she hadn't thought to put on make-up—a touch of lip balm, perhaps, but nothing more.

Lucy was thankful she had chosen to dress sensibly, in the freshly laundered clothes in which she had left the palace: a simple pair of cotton trousers, and a tailored shirt rolled up to the elbows. The very last thing she wanted was to cut a frivolous figure. She was a down-to-earth working mother, and she had no intention of behaving like an impostor to please her desert prince. Kahlil would have to accept her for who she was; there could be no compromise ever where that was concerned.

Lucy tensed as, having finished his conversation, Kahlil turned to her. Resplendent in his desert robes, with soft silk trousers showing beneath, he looked every inch the future ruler of Abadan. There was purpose to his stride as he came quickly towards her. The moment Edward saw his father crossing the sand towards them he started bunny-hopping with excitement. And, in spite of both Lucy's and Safia's best efforts, he refused to quieten down.

Taking the steps two at a time, Kahlil came over and, without a word to Lucy, claimed his son, sweeping him high into the air above his head. Holding him aloft, he turned to look down on the thousands of people gathered in front of him.

The massed tribesmen raised their fists high and gave a deep-throated roar of approval that ran a chill down Lucy's spine. Edward had been claimed as one of them, she realised, feeling a confusing mixture of pride and fear. There could be no turning back now.

CHAPTER ELEVEN

THEY ate a delicious meal, sitting cross-legged on cushions beneath the shady canopy. A vast selection of delicacies was brought to them, and the feast didn't draw to a conclusion until purple shadows had started to track across the mustard-coloured sand.

Kahlil devoted most of his time to Edward—and, though Lucy was growing to enjoy watching them together because it made Edward so happy, she was becoming increasingly frustrated, sure Kahlil was deliberately evading her attempts to pin him down about the future.

'There are some people I must talk to when we have finished eating,' he said when coffee was being served. 'Edward should leave us now. It will be tedious for him to have to sit still and listen.'

'But I thought *we* were going to talk,' Lucy said, conscious that the nursemaid was already moving to take Edward back to the women's tent. She was torn, seeing how tired Edward was, but knowing she would never be ready to accept Kahlil's orders where he was concerned. Moving to go with them, Lucy was surprised when Kahlil touched her arm, stopping her.

'Edward is tired,' he said. 'The women can see to him. You can go to him later.'

'But you have things to do here,' she pointed out. 'Surely it would be better if I went with Edward?'

'We still have things to talk about, and Edward will sleep now. There is nothing more you can do for him tonight.'

'But I'd rather go with him—'

'Sit down. Please, Lucy.' Kahlil's voice dropped a tone.

128

Reluctant to make a scene in front of all the tribesmen, Lucy settled back onto the cushions, watching Safia take Edward into the women's tent, and noticing Kahlil was doing the same.

'Before we talk, I must greet some of the elders of the tribe,' Kahlil explained the moment Edward had disappeared from sight. 'I will share a glass of tea with them as our custom demands.'

'When will we talk?' Lucy pressed.

'As soon as this is over. If you would rather wait for me inside the pavilion—?'

'No, this is fine,' Lucy said. 'I'll stay here.' Kahlil's way of life fascinated her. This was a great opportunity to learn more about the father of her son. 'Would you like me to move back,' she offered, 'so that you can speak to the other men in private?'

'I have nothing to hide,' Kahlil said dryly, 'and neither do my kinsmen. You may stay where you are.'

Lucy's pulse quickened when his hard mouth softened in the suggestion of a smile. And he was in no hurry to look away. It was she who broke eye contact first, her heart racing as her mind flashed back to their earlier passion. She could almost believe there was something more between them than their son and sexual attraction. She wanted to believe...

Then Kahlil turned away and made a sign to one of his attendants. At his signal, the line of men waiting at the foot of the stairs began moving slowly towards them.

'What did he mean?' Lucy said, turning to Kahlil as the last of the elderly tribesmen made a deep bow towards them both. 'Who is Nurse Clemmy?' She broke off to smile at the older man as he left them to join the others. He had stared at her throughout the audience with Kahlil, exclaiming in Abadanese under his breath, and then, when he'd spoken directly to Kahlil, had repeated the name 'Nurse Clemmy' over and over as he gestured towards her, his eyes bright with excitement.

'Nurse Clemmy was my mother,' Kahlil said. 'Ahmed Mehdi Bhaya has noted the resemblance between the two of you, as have many of the people here.'

'I look like your mother?'

'You are the same type of woman,' he said, in a way that made Lucy wonder whether that was a good thing or not.

Determined, stubborn, and as spirited as my most troublesome thoroughbred, Kahlil was thinking, counting himself fortunate that Lucy could not read his thoughts. But he could see she was burning up with curiosity.

'So your mother was a nurse?'

'Yes, she was.'

There was something in Kahlil's eyes that made Lucy hesitate before pressing on. 'I don't mean to pry—if you'd rather not talk about her...'

As he turned his luminous dark eyes on her Lucy felt their power through every inch of her body.

'Of course I like to talk about her. Ask me anything you like.'

'How did she meet your father?' Lucy asked, her brow wrinkling in thought as she remembered the old standard lamp in the ruling Sheikh's quarters and his father's explanation for it...There were so many clues, and now she was wishing she had picked up on them sooner, given the older man a chance to talk about his Western wife.

'She nursed him in hospital,' Kahlil said, reclaiming her attention. 'Something of a cliché,' he admitted dryly. 'But that's where everything predictable finishes and the true love story begins.'

He had Lucy totally hooked now. She was barely aware that the servants had backed away discreetly and, with the tribesmen already heading for their trucks and their camels, they were completely alone. 'Go on,' she murmured, her gaze locked on Kahlil's face.

'She was older than my father,' he said, his face softening as he gazed into the fiery haze of the desert sunset. 'She broke every convention when he brought her back here. Not only was she an older woman, but she insisted on continuing her work during her marriage to the ruling Sheikh of Abadan—something that had never been heard of before Nurse Clemmy came along.'

'She sounds like quite a woman.'

'She was.'

'What happened?' Lucy said softly, but seeing the look in Kahlil's eyes she already dreaded his answer.

'An accident in the desert,' he said flatly. 'She was trying to save the life of a child who had fallen down a ravine.' He looked away and flinched, as if the memory caused him actual physical pain. 'She should never have been out in the desert on her own.'

Anger had begun to colour his voice, and Lucy felt a stab of guilt knowing her own reckless act had only rekindled terrible memories for him. 'I'm sorry,' she said, knowing it wasn't enough.

'I thought my father would never get over it...' Kahlil stopped and eased his shoulders in a shrug. 'Our people believe she is an angel now, looking down on them, guarding them and protecting them from harm—even arranging their marriages for them.' His lips twisted halfway between a grimace and a smile.

'She sounds like a saint.'

'A saint with her feet firmly on the ground, as well as a wicked sense of humour,' he said, lightening a little. 'She always said she needed a sense of humour to survive her name.'

'Her name?'

'Clementine Ballantine.'

'It sounds like her parents had the sense of humour,' Lucy said, smiling.

'She insisted on being called Clemmy, and took herself off to college, where she trained to become a nurse. Then she fell in love with my father and came to live here in Abadan.'

'You said she continued to work?'

'She revolutionised our medical system, and brought forward the cause of Abadanese women by several hundred years.'

So what had gone wrong? How had such a wonderful legacy been allowed to slip away? What a tragedy that no one had picked up Nurse Clemmy's torch. And now it was too late, Lucy mused, looking at Kahlil. Neither he nor his father would ever allow things to go back to the way they had been when Nurse Clemmy was alive.

They were still bitter that Nurse Clemmy had left them, she realised suddenly, softening towards Kahlil as she felt his pain. Why could life never be simple? Why was the black and white of their relationship, the reasons behind their battle for custody of Edward, growing indistinct? Why did she have to care for Kahlil so much?

'She sounds like a great woman,' Lucy said sincerely. 'I wish I could have known her.'

'She *was* a great woman,' Kahlil murmured distantly. 'Truly great.'

How they ended up in each other's arms Lucy wasn't quite sure. There was a moment when she was following Kahlil's stare out into the deepening shadows, and then another when she was kissing him as if it was the most natural thing in the world…something they both wanted, both needed equally.

'We'll talk?' Lucy whispered when he released her at last.

'Later,' Kahlil promised. Standing up, he drew her to her feet.

The moon cast a silver net across the bed, bathing Lucy's flushed face in light. She wondered if Kahlil could ever get enough of her, or she of him... They were both insatiable, she decided, running her fingertips through his thick glossy hair as he moved steadily down the bed, kissing every inch of her along the way.

He had taught her the Eastern way of making love... drawing out the pleasure until she reached another level of consciousness—one that took her far beyond her worldly concerns and into another place, where pleasure ruled and sensation was everything. She felt safe, and happy, and completely loved. Reality couldn't intrude here, she thought, sighing in anticipation of pleasure as he eased her thighs apart. Kahlil could do more with his tongue than any man could hope to achieve in a lifetime of fumbling...and his hands—

Lucy cried out as he cupped her buttocks and brought her beneath him. 'Again?' she murmured with surprise.

'I'm only just getting warmed up,' he promised, slanting her a smile before claiming her mouth again with a deep, passionate kiss.

They belonged together; they were made for each other... The words in Lucy's head were borne out by Kahlil's actions, and those actions were clearing her mind of thought so that now she could only move with him, rhythmically, deeply and steadily, putting every bit of her strength behind the thrust of her hips, the clutch of her fingers as she held on to his shoulders.

With a deep groan of satisfaction Kahlil rolled away from her when they were spent. 'You are a wildcat,' he murmured, staring at the battle wounds on his arms. But he didn't seem concerned as he reached for her and brought her close. 'I cannot get enough of you,' he murmured, and Lucy thought she detected an element of surprise in his voice as he turned to plant a tender kiss on her face. 'Soon I may not be able to live without you at all.'

He stopped when Lucy shifted position to stare at him in astonishment. 'You really care for me?'

'Of course I care for you,' he said impatiently. 'And that is why I am able to say this to you—'

'What?' Lucy whispered tenderly, brushing a lock of hair back from his face. This was the man she wanted for the father of her son; this was the man she knew she could love. 'What do you want to say to me, Kahlil?'

'I want to talk to you about getting married.'

'Getting married?' Lucy breathed in astonishment. 'But Kahlil—'

'For Edward's sake,' he broke in, staring deep into her eyes as he brought her hand to his lips. 'You cannot be my mistress, Lucy. Edward's parents must be married.'

Elation ripped through Lucy, transporting her to a place she had only dreamed of before. But when she looked into Kahlil's eyes, expecting some mirror image of her own heated emotion, she saw there was nothing. She made a small sound of uncertainty, frowning, suspended in a type of limbo. Like a feather on a breath of wind, she felt her emotions could be tossed either way.

'Edward must be legitimate if he is to inherit the throne of Abadan one day,' Kahlil explained, sitting up as practical matters took over his thoughts.

'I see...'

'So I am proposing that we get married—what do you think?'

Lucy swallowed, giving herself time to collect her thoughts. She wanted to feel as any other woman might feel at such a moment: elated, overjoyed, maybe even a little disbelieving, but absolutely sure, absolutely confident. But she was not confident. She was anything but confident. There was something Kahlil wasn't saying. He had begun with a proposal when there should have been a few words of preparation first, or a special look, a lingering touch. There had been nothing.

Lucy searched his face to be sure, but there was absolutely no emotion in Kahlil's eyes. He had made her a practical proposition, and now she was expected to answer him.

'It would only be for a short while, of course,' he said, as if he thought that would offer her some encouragement. 'I'd have a proper contract drawn up. Let's say six months?' His mouth tugged down enquiringly as he looked at her.

Six months. Enough time to establish Edward's legitimacy before admitting to the world they'd made a mistake.

'Come now, Lucy—surely you can see what a good idea it is?' he said when she still remained silent. 'I'm not asking anything of you.'

'You're...not...asking...anything...of...me?' Lucy repeated, finding it hard to breathe, feeling as if a leather strap had just been tightened around her chest. 'Is that what you think, Kahlil?'

She sprang away from him as he went to touch her, landing on the floor awkwardly and shaking him off when he lunged forward to steady her. Grabbing the sheet, feeling her nakedness like a towering shame, Lucy wrapped it tightly around her.

'And after six months?' she said, her face white with shock, her eyes glittering with disbelief. 'What then, Kahlil?'

'That's when I release you,' he said soothingly, swinging off the bed to go and comfort her.

'Get away from me!' Lucy warned, taking a step back. Snatching up his robe from a chair, she flung it at him. 'Put this on. I can't bear to look at you.'

Kahlil frowned, suddenly conscious that he too was naked. Slipping the robe over his head, he gazed down at her, all the majesty of his position safely restored. 'Before you cast any more accusations at me,' he said, 'won't you listen to what I have to say?'

'I'll listen,' Lucy said tensely, facing him. She was not going to give him the satisfaction of breaking down. She forced her breathing to steady, and straightened up so he would see she couldn't be intimidated.

'We will get married,' Kahlil began, confident of her agreement. 'Edward will be made legitimate and recognised by the Council as my heir. And then, in six months' time, I will grant you a divorce. You will be free, Lucy. Free to do as you please. You know I would never stop you seeing Edward. I understand how much you love him.'

It was too much. Lucy almost broke down. She had no idea how she managed to keep her eyeline steady and the tears safely locked behind her frozen stare. She doubted Kahlil had the slightest idea about love, let alone how much love she had for Edward. And as for the love she had for the man standing before her? That was the real tragedy, Lucy thought, listening but not hearing as Kahlil continued to put his case for a marriage of convenience. Sheikh Kahlil of Abadan had broken her heart, and nothing he could do to her now would ever cause her more pain.

'I don't want to raise any false hope,' Kahlil said encouragingly, as if he sensed Lucy's disappointment. 'You must see that you could never sit on the throne of Abadan at my side—we will have to divorce. But we will live out of the public eye, I promise you. I would never subject you to gossip, or cruel innuendo. People will hardly know what has taken place—the upheaval for you will be minimal.'

And at that point Lucy almost hit him. Anger welled from deep inside her as she faced up to him. She was good enough to bear Sheikh Kahlil's child, but not good enough to sit beside him on the throne of Abadan.

But what good would anger do? she wondered, feeling her fury quickly overtaken by despair. For Edward's sake she would do this. For Edward's sake she would marry the man she loved and then be humiliated by him after six short months, when he divorced her in front of the entire world.

Lucy looked at Kahlil as if seeing him clearly for the first time. Even now she couldn't hate him. She could only love him. And if six months was all Kahlil had to offer, then she would take six months.

'I'll go further,' Kahlil offered when Lucy remained silent. 'You can go home with Edward—as soon as you like. Breathing space,' he explained, opening his arms in an expansive gesture. 'This has been a tremendous shock for all of us. I can see you need time. You *should* have time,' he said decisively, 'and I'm going to give you all the time you need.'

Lucy couldn't prevent the small sound of contradiction escaping her throat, and was glad that Kahlil was so determined to convince her that he had come up with an acceptable plan he didn't notice. There could never be enough time to come to terms with what was happening.

'When will we go?' she heard herself say. A sense of unreality swept over her. Going home was what she wanted more than anything—wasn't it? But now the moment had come the thought of leaving Abadan filled her with dread. Then Edward swam into her mind—she would be with him—her face softened.

'That's better. I was beginning to think I would never see you smile again.'

Was she smiling? Lucy wondered. The whole episode had shocked her so much she had no control over her responses

'I know this must all seem contrived to you,' Kahlil said. 'But Edward cannot be my heir under the laws of Abadan unless and until we are married. That is a fact, and there is nothing that either of us can do about it. I take it you want Edward to inherit the throne of Abadan in due course?'

His gaze rested on her face but Lucy's mind went blank.

This wasn't the battle she had intended to fight—a clean-cut legal contest to secure custody of Edward. This had turned into something heart-rending and ghastly, something unbelievably bitter and disappointing. 'Marriage...' she murmured distractedly.

'Our relationship must be legalised, recognised here in Abadan.'

'Our *relationship*?' The word grated on her. 'Don't you mean sex?'

'Don't cheapen what we have, Lucy,' Khalil said, frowning. 'I'm just stating facts plainly. I can see you need time to think about this, but you don't need to worry, I'll get my legal team onto it straight away. And if you have any difficulty locating a lawyer to act for you I'm sure I can help—'

'No, thank you,' Lucy said, quickly reclaiming her composure. 'I'm quite capable of handling that side of things myself.'

'If you're certain?'

'I'm positive.'

'Lucy,' Kahlil said, moving closer until he could brush aside the hair that had fallen over her face. 'Come here to me.'

Inwardly spent, Lucy moved like a rag doll and Kahlil brought her back into his arms. 'Surely you can see that we both need some time apart?' he murmured.

And then he nuzzled his face against her cheek, and she felt his warmth, inhaled his special scent, and tears began to trickle unhindered down her cheeks. Was this how the Sheikh disposed of a mistress when he was tired of her? Lucy supposed she should count herself fortunate. Kahlil was offering her marriage for the sake of their son. And he didn't have to. He must love Edward very much, she realised.

'I'll go and shower and dress,' she said, wiping her eyes discreetly, 'and then we can finalise the details.'

CHAPTER TWELVE

Lucy's cottage in Westbury on a freezing cold March morning was quite literally a world away from the sultry romance of a desert encampment. And as for the Golden Palace—that seemed nothing more than a mirage in the desert, like everything else in Abadan.

Throwing back the curtains, she stared out at the main street running through the village. The road was glittering with frost, making the desert seem further away than ever. Abadan seemed nothing more now than a fantasy kingdom that only the most inventive film director might have dreamed up.

At least Westbury Hall looked magnificent after its face-lift. The work on the building was almost completed. Her own dreams might have been crushed, but she was glad someone else had taken up the challenge. Rumour said it had been turned into a luxury hotel and spa, and it did seem the most likely explanation that a leisure complex had been built. There was even a helicopter landing pad on the newly reinforced roof.

As Edward claimed her attention Lucy saw how close he was to walking unaided, and felt a flash of regret that Kahlil wouldn't be there to see his son's first steps. But Kahlil had made his choice and he had to live with it, just as she had to face the prospect of a loveless marriage.

Not loveless on her part, Lucy thought, feeling frustration sweep over her. She was in control of every other area of her life, but where Kahlil was concerned she seemed to have lost touch with reality. He had no love for her and it was time to accept that fact. Their marriage would be one of expedience only.

And thanks to Kahlil she also had silent visitors to contend with. His security forces were always around—and not just the man lodged in her guest bedroom. There were more, she noticed, parked across the road in a discreet black sedan. She could pick them out easily.

Turning away from the window to prepare Edward's breakfast, Lucy couldn't help thinking about their forthcoming marriage. It had turned her into something of a celebrity in the village, as well as the envy of her friends. Only she knew the reality of the situation. There wasn't much romance in a marriage of convenience. And with the bodyguards part of her life now she was just as much a prisoner in Westbury as she had been captive to the Sheikh in Abadan. Kahlil could control events even from half a world away, Lucy realised, making a point of smiling at Edward when she realised he was watching her.

She had to guard her feelings all the time. She was determined Edward would never suffer because of the lack of love between his parents. Nor would he ever know the humiliation she felt at being deemed an unsuitable consort for the Crown Prince of Abadan. She was good enough for a marriage of subterfuge and concealment, good enough stock to provide Kahlil with an heir, but not good enough to uphold the dignity of the throne of Abadan.

Lucy jumped with surprise as the doorbell rang, and for one crazy, exhilarating moment she felt sure it would be Kahlil at the door. Rushing to peer out of the hall window, she saw it was only the mail delivery man with a large package.

Disappointment and relief swept over her in turn as she hurried to open the door. Had she really thought Sheikh Kahlil of Abadan would simply turn up unannounced on her doorstep, like any ordinary mortal?

'What on earth's this?' Lucy exclaimed as the man carried the large carton into the narrow hallway for her.

'Beats me,' he said. 'Sign here, please. I've got three
more for you in the van.'

'Three more!' Lucy knew in her heart where they must
have come from.

When the man had left, she sank down on the floor beside
the boxes. The only thing that stopped her breaking down
was Edward. She was determined not to let him see his
mother crying over what she knew would almost certainly
be her wedding dress and accessories.

In the first carton Lucy discovered a fabulous jewelled
veil covered in crystals and pearls. Holding it up to the light,
she felt sure it must be meant for someone else because it
was so beautiful. Even with the evidence of the clothes she
would wear on her wedding day surrounding her, marriage
to Kahlil had never seemed more unreal.

When she had opened all three boxes, and rifled through
the reams of tissue paper, Lucy sat back on her haunches.
Kahlil had bought her after all—and for the price of a dress
and a few trinkets.

'For the photographs,' his accompanying letter assured
her. 'It wouldn't do for Edward to think his parents' marriage a hastily arranged affair.'

Kahlil was right again. There was no reason why Edward
should be short-changed just because his mother had made
such a hash of things. And his father was arriving tomorrow,
Lucy saw, reading on.

Crumpling up the page, she held it to her breast. She felt
weak just thinking about Kahlil's arrival. She never knew
what to expect from him, or what he was thinking. One day
maybe someone would strip away his defences, get to know
the real man, but it wouldn't be her, however much she
longed to. She had tried and failed to get beneath his steely
façade.

'Come on, young man,' she said, turning to Edward, who was already delving into the boxes and scattering clothes and shoes everywhere. 'There's nothing for you in here.'

Except for a box-load of memories for when you are older, Lucy thought as she swept her son into her arms. *And then you'll have to make of them what you will. Because I won't be able to elaborate on whatever fantasy your imagination conjures up. Nor will I be able to make palatable the fact that your parents married and then divorced within the space of a few months.*

Taking Edward into the kitchen to make them both breakfast, she carried on reading. There would be a discreet civil service at Westbury Hall, Kahlil had written. So it was to be a hotel, Lucy thought, glancing out of the kitchen window. She couldn't ignore the irony—both 'Kahl' and her ambitious plans for Westbury Hall had proved a disaster, and now she was to be married at the Hall, to Kahl!

From practically every room in her small cottage Lucy had some view of Westbury Hall. That was how the idea of renovating the magnificent old building had taken such a hold in the first place. She couldn't tear her gaze away from it now, knowing her wedding was to be held there. Hopefully the decorators would be out in time—but, knowing Kahlil's influence extended far beyond the boundaries of Abadan, she didn't doubt the new owners of the Hall would make sure everything was ready for him.

While she was warming Edward's milk Lucy spotted another van turning in through the Hall's imposing gates and felt a fierce pang of regret. She had so wanted to bring the old place back to life, but the challenge had got away from her—rather like that other challenge she had encountered at the Hall, the one that had called himself Kahl.

The rest of the day passed in a whirlwind of activity. Lucy had booked into the local beauty salon for a manicure, a facial and a massage. It might be a waste of time, but there was no reason not to look her best when Sheikh Kahlil of Abadan turned up on the doorstep.

Later, when Edward was sleeping, Lucy crept up the stairs and went into the nursery just to look down at him. He looked like a sleeping fawn, innocent and untroubled, with his baby hands curled up as if he was holding her finger—or his father's. Backing away, she hugged herself, shutting her eyes tightly for a moment. The only time she ever saw Kahlil soften was when he was with Edward, and then she saw a very different side of the desert Prince— someone who might almost have made a good family man—

'Don't be ridiculous!' Lucy muttered impatiently. It was time she stopped behaving like a romantic fool where Kahlil was concerned.

Leaving the nursery on tiptoe, Lucy left the door ajar so she could hear Edward through the night. Returning downstairs, she went into her study and closed the curtains, shutting out the cold, bleak night. All her important papers were still on top of her desk, where she had left them. The marriage contract her lawyers had asked her to sign took pride of place.

She had refused all payment for herself, and Kahlil had respected that. But she knew that everything Edward could possibly need would be provided for most generously. There would be regular trips between Abadan and Westbury, and they would spend more time in Westbury than Lucy had dared to hope. Leila was to be given the job of full-time nanny—which, in Lucy's opinion as well as Kahlil's, would provide additional stability for Edward.

Kahlil had thought of everything—except love, Lucy reflected, laying down the fountain pen she had just picked up. She didn't want to read it, couldn't quite bring herself to sign such a cold-blooded document. But as long as Kahlil loved Edward, that was all that mattered.

Lucy knew the only thing she wanted, the only thing she had a right to expect was joint custody of their son. Kahlil had already agreed to grant her that without a fight. She should be satisfied. But still she was restless without knowing why.

Beginning to shiver, she saw the fire had burned low in the grate. She was glad to have something practical to do. Adding more coal, she stirred the fire into life again with a brass poker, and then sat back on her heels. 'Very soon I will be a wife—and a princess,' she said aloud, on a note of incredulity. The word *princess* was so alien to her it filled her with apprehension. 'And then, in six months' time, or even less, I will be a free woman again,' she added firmly for reassurance.

The whole marriage machine would roll on with or without her co-operation. Kahlil's staff were making all the arrangements. 'Perfect. Saves me the trouble,' she whispered, biting back tears.

Kahlil will be here today, was Lucy's first thought on waking. She was grateful for Edward's routine. It gave her something to do other than stare out of the window every five minutes.

His letter had said he would be with them by nine o'clock. So by eight Lucy was building towers with Edward out of plastic containers on the kitchen table. The table just happened to be by a window that looked over the road.

Edward saw him first—or rather he saw the sleek black limousine that drew up outside. And then Kahlil was out of the car and striding up the path almost before it had drawn to a halt. Lucy's heart was hammering so hard in her chest it hurt. She had forgotten how tall he was, how powerful. Even in the dark, formal suit he looked so regal.

She stayed out of sight, watching as he stopped before the porch to take in the cottage with one sweeping glance.

There was just a touch of humour in his eyes, she noticed with surprise, and she flushed pink as she realised that he was remembering everything about their first encounter— but Edward was jiggling up and down in her arms, eager to greet his father.

'Just a minute, please,' Lucy said to Edward firmly, watching Kahlil turn to stare at Westbury Hall. Of course— that was where it had all begun for both of them. Her heart lurched as he turned back to the cottage and reached for the doorbell.

She remembered everything too, Lucy thought on her way to the door. Every time she walked past the gates of the Hall. And every time she felt the same thrill, the same certainty that she had done nothing wrong. She smiled at Edward as she reached the front door. 'How could it be wrong when I have you?' she whispered in his ear.

The bodyguard Kahlil insisted upon, who lived in the house alongside them, like a wraith, descended the stairs like a cannonball. Stretching one arm out in front of Lucy, he swung the door open and bowed low. Heat streamed into Lucy's veins. She was glad of Edward's comforting warmth in her arms as she stood back in the shadows with him, waiting. There was a great gust of fresh air laced with cinnamon and ginger as Kahlil stepped into the tiny hall.

'Lucy,' he said, looking down at her.

Here in the low-beamed cottage, standing in the shady hall, he seemed immense, magnificent. Sheikh Kahlil of Abadan had an immense presence, Lucy thought, steeling herself to meet his gaze. She had prepared herself for this moment. She would expect nothing and therefore could not be disappointed. That was what she had told herself. But she was disappointed. There was nothing—nothing at all between them, she realised as he swept a frantically excited Edward out of her arms.

'My son!' he exclaimed softly and emotionally, holding Edward close for a moment.

She could never have truly prepared herself for this, Lucy realised, seeing the look in Edward's eyes as he gazed into his father's face. Not for the great well of longing that opened up in her heart. But what had she been expecting? That they would both be swept into Kahlil's arms like a proper family? That she would be greeted like Kahlil's future wife, with love and tender kisses in the expectation of a lifetime of happiness together?

'Did you have a good journey?' she said, forcing the traditional courtesy through her lips.

Kahlil frowned briefly. 'I could have brought the helicopter,' he said, and there was an edge of irritation in his voice as he glanced over his shoulder through the mullioned window at Westbury Hall. 'I didn't realise they'd finished the roof.'

Lucy stared up at him in bewilderment. His comment was so far distant from her own thoughts that it took her a moment to respond. 'That would have been more convenient for you,' she said at last, not sure that he was listening.

'Shall we go in?' he said, looking beyond Lucy, deeper into the cottage.

'Yes—yes, of course,' she said, backing down the hallway in front of him. 'You've had a long trip. Won't you come into the kitchen for a coffee, tea…some breakfast?'

There was something unreal about inviting the imposing figure of Sheikh Kahlil of Abadan into her humble kitchen for coffee. But Kahl hadn't been too proud to eat and drink in her kitchen almost two years ago, Lucy remembered, watching him set Edward down on his play rug.

'You've made some changes,' Kahlil observed.

'For Edward's safety,' Lucy said. She was glad to turn her back and busy herself at the Aga with the kettle and two mugs. 'This thing gets red-hot,' she turned to explain, 'so I had a guard frame with a gate made to fit around it. But it won't be long until he learns how to open it— Edward!' she exclaimed, putting the mugs down again.

Kahlil too stood frozen to the spot as Edward took his first few faltering steps unaided. Arms outstretched, he staggered determinedly towards his father and finally, in triumph, grabbed hold of Kahlil's legs.

Lucy's hand flew to her chest and she drew a deep, steadying breath. 'I'm so glad you were here for that,' she said honestly.

'So am I,' Kahlil said, his voice hoarse with emotion as he lifted Edward into his arms.

Briefly, Lucy turned away, not wanting to begrudge either of them such a special moment. But she was tormented by the fear that every step Edward took towards his father was a step away from her.

When Edward called for her attention a flood of fresh resolve came over her and she hurried to share his excitement, not caring that when she hugged Edward she was forced hard against Kahlil. There might be nothing left between them, but this was a very special moment.

Kahlil suggested Edward should be taken for a walk in his stroller. 'Don't look so worried, Lucy. I brought a friend of yours and Edward's with me from Abadan,' he said, looking towards the door.

'Leila!' Lucy said, exclaiming with pleasure when she saw the girl. 'It's so good to see you.'

'And you,' Leila said warmly. 'Shall I take Edward now?' She came in to collect her charge.

'You do seem to have thought of everything,' Lucy admitted, turning to Kahlil, conscious that Edward was reaching out for his father, reluctant to leave him now.

'Edward loves his daddy—don't you, Edward?' Leila said fondly, piercing Lucy's heart with her innocent words. 'But we could go and feed the ducks, if you like?'

Her distraction was skilful, and Edward was easily persuaded. Lucy could already feel Kahlil's influence pushing
them both this way and that, and he had only been back in
their lives a few minutes.

'Do all the clothes that I had sent over for the wedding
fit?' Kahlil asked, when the door had closed behind Leila
and Edward.

'Perfectly,' Lucy said tensely, finding her gaze drawn
against her will to his strong, tanned fingers—fingers that
had measured every inch of her with such accuracy.

'Good.'

As their gazes met and held Lucy turned away, feeling
awkward. She wasn't sure what Kahlil expected of her. 'I've
already picked up some of my old contacts,' she said, forcing a bright conversational note into her voice. 'I should be
quite busy after the wedding.'

'What do you mean?' he said sharply.

'I mean I'll start work right away...'

Kahlil swore softly in his own tongue. 'Are you mad?'
he said in English, staring at Lucy in amazement.

'You always knew I would keep on working. It's written
into the contract on my desk. We agreed—'

'You *shall* work,' Kahlil said, 'but not here—not in this
country. I have much to occupy me in Abadan. You must
be with me for much of the time, and I would not expect
you to sit around all day doing nothing. My people expect—'

'*Our* people—if only for six months,' Lucy reminded
him, trying to stay cool, trying to be reasonable.

'Our people,' he conceded—but grudgingly, Lucy
thought. 'The people of Abadan will expect to see us together, performing certain official duties.'

Lucy's patience was wearing thin. He seemed to have
everything worked out in advance. She hadn't been con-

sulted about anything. 'Isn't that a little modern?' she interrupted, stung into a sharp retort by his manner.

'Not for me,' Kahlil said, 'and not for the people of Abadan. Why, Lucy? Don't you think you can handle it?'

'I can handle it,' Lucy said, feeling her anger mounting. She was determined not to be backed into the place Kahlil wanted her to be: the willing wife, the obedient consort, the woman without a mind of her own, the person who could be swept up and dropped at will, whenever and wherever it pleased him.

'Good, then that's settled. After the wedding tomorrow—'

'Tomorrow!'

'Is there any reason to wait?'

'In Abadan you said I needed time,' Lucy exclaimed, springing to her feet. 'You said we both did. You promised I would have all the time I needed to come to terms with this.'

'I had to bring things forward; I have responsibilities. The formalities are being arranged.'

'Everything is being arranged from the sound of it,' Lucy said tensely.

'The guests have been informed; none of them has complained,' Kahlil pointed out impatiently. 'I can't see why you should be so reluctant.'

'Oh, really?' Lucy said shaking her head. 'This is my life we're talking about, Kahlil, and I won't be controlled by you.'

'You will do whatever is necessary.'

'I will do anything for Edward,' Lucy agreed. 'But if you think for one moment you can order me around, that I will become your bond slave the moment we're married, you're mistaken. I agreed to this marriage for Edward—not for myself, and certainly not for you!'

'Nevertheless, we will be married tomorrow,' Kahlil said,

standing up to face her. 'And immediately after the wedding you and Edward will accompany me to Abadan.'

Lucy couldn't believe what she was hearing. She had been so sure there would be more time. She had been complacent—too complacent, she realised now.

'There will be a civil ceremony tomorrow, here at Westbury Hall,' Kahlil continued remorselessly. 'That is so our marriage will be recognised in your country. When we return to Abadan we will have a second ceremony—a blessing, if you like—so that my people can greet and accept my new wife.'

Unable to meet his eyes, Lucy looked at her hands and found they were shaking. 'I didn't realise... I mean, I didn't think Edward and I would be leaving for Abadan straight after the wedding.'

Kahlil moved a step towards her, as if he thought she needed some reassurance.

'Don't,' Lucy said. 'Don't touch me. I can't believe you're trying to rush me into marriage like this.'

'Rush you?' Kahlil queried coldly. 'We agreed for Edward's sake.'

'Yes, we agreed, but you said it would happen when I was ready.'

'It can't wait for ever, and the time is convenient.'

'For whom?' But Lucy knew she was wasting her breath. And she *had* agreed. She wouldn't back down. 'Very well, but I won't be manipulated again.'

'Manipulated?'

'First Westbury Hall, and now our marriage...'

'Westbury Hall?' Kahlil said, watching her carefully.

'Yes,' Lucy said, unable to subdue her suspicions any longer. 'You were up to something, weren't you?' She stopped, seeing his face, and knew she had hit a nerve. 'So I am right,' she said, wishing at once it wasn't true. 'What did you really come for that day? What were you up to?

Did you have a property developer in your pocket? Or did you tip off the consortium that bought it? Or did you simply want to steal my ideas for the renovation?'

'Your ideas were always in the public domain.'

'Westbury Hall means nothing to you,' Lucy said bitterly. 'It was just a game as far as you were concerned—one you had to win.' He couldn't deny it, she gathered, when he remained silent. 'You'll never know what Westbury Hall means to me. I loved the old lady who lived there—my parents worked for her all their lives. We loved her, and Lady Grace loved us—' Lucy stopped, hearing her voice break. 'But why do I expect you to understand? You don't know what love is, do you, Kahlil? You don't have the slightest idea. You just take charge of people's lives—that's what you're good at. You have no respect for anyone. I was just a little bonus on top of whatever deal you were making.'

'I'll go now.' Kahlil's voice was as steady as if they were two strangers parting on the best of terms. 'I'm sure you must have preparations to make for our marriage tomorrow.'

Marriage! She didn't know how he could bring himself to mention it so casually.

'I trust any business meetings you may have arranged can be postponed?' he said, pausing on his way to the door.

'Yes, of course,' Lucy managed distractedly, still in turmoil.

'Excellent,' Kahlil said, striding out without a backward glance.

She felt faint, light-headed, and quite suddenly nothing seemed real. She felt as if she had just been swept up in a whirlwind and had landed somewhere she couldn't recognise, where she didn't have the skills to survive.

Lucy steeled herself as she prepared to leave the horse-drawn carriage. Kahlil had insisted upon a carriage, even though her cottage was only a few steps from the Hall. He said she must be driven around the village so that people could see her, and so that photographs of the occasion could be taken for Edward's sake. And she had agreed. She didn't want Edward thinking his parents' marriage had been loveless when he grew older. It was far better for him to believe it had been a fairytale that had lost its way.

As one of Kahlil's men stepped forward to help her negotiate the steps Lucy lifted her head to acknowledge him. He was another of the silent men she was becoming used to—interchangeable, like chess pieces, but a lot more deadly. She already felt the subtle change in her position as he stood at her side. It wasn't human kindness that made the man reach out to steady her as she lifted her skirts and picked her way carefully—it was his bounden duty now to protect her from harm.

The harness clinked behind her as the horses stamped their feet and blew down their noses, impatient to be gone. But there was no escape for her, Lucy thought, shivering in the biting wind.

Straightening the folds of her dress, she looked up as the doors of the Hall swung open to admit her. A rush of warmth and light and sound spilled out as she started up the steps. She was glad to have the posy in her hands to cling to. She had insisted on choosing the flowers for her wedding bouquet—simple blooms from the local greenhouse: jonquil, freesia and some early tulips. She had bound them herself with some supple young strands of curving purple willow. It trailed below ribbons she had laced around her fingers.

Her hands were pale and shaking, Lucy noticed, keeping her head down to concentrate on the jewelled satin slippers on her feet. The slippers belonged in a fairytale, as did the ivory satin cape lined with soft fur she was wearing over her intricately beaded wedding dress. But this was not her fairytale. She was an impostor.

She would not turn back. She would not allow anything to stand in the way of Edward's future happiness.

Kahlil's evasion the previous day still rankled, but Lucy had found a way to cope with the farce that was her wedding day. She would enjoy the luxurious feel of cool silks and satin against her naked skin as an actress might. She would relish the scent of French perfume as the couture clothes brushed her legs just as if she had donned some lovely new costume to play a part.

And that was all she was doing, Lucy reassured herself as she stepped over the threshold of Westbury Hall. She was playing a role for Edward's sake. And she would play it well.

Raising her head proudly, she saw Kahlil, waiting for her with Edward beside him in Leila's arms. And then she became aware of many more people, most of whom she didn't know.

Some she did—friends from the village, from her schooldays, from her college, and both close and extended family. Kahlil had gone to endless trouble, Lucy registered with surprise, wondering how on earth everyone had been assembled in time.

And then there were others—dignitaries from a host of foreign countries, with ribbons, and medals, and sashes, and jewels—all waiting for her arrival! It seemed quite incredible—impossible.

Swallowing hard, Lucy tried to move forward, but her earlier confidence had deserted her and her feet seemed rooted to the spot. Then Kahlil was beside her and her frozen hand was enveloped in his. He felt so warm and steady. She allowed him to lead her forward, slowly and carefully, as if she was a precious item that might crumble if he handled her too firmly.

But as soon as he felt her strength return he released her again, and Lucy knew it would have been better if he had left her to blunder around until some dutiful member of staff brought her to him. His consideration only made her more aware that, with good cause to hate him, she was in love with him. Sheikh Kahlil of Abadan was more than just the father of her son: he was the only man she would ever love. Her world, Lucy realised with a great burst of emotion. But as far as Kahlil was concerned she was merely a convenient wife, the woman who had supplied him with a son.

Lucy kept her head throughout the ceremony, behaving impeccably, responding when required, and even smiling up at Kahlil as if she didn't have a care in the world later, when they danced together. She would have forgiven his indifference towards her in an instant, forgotten every one of her suspicions about him for just one word of tenderness—one look, or one smile, something intimate and private passing between them. But he behaved towards her like a very courteous and considerate stranger.

When he finally escorted her back to her seat at the high table, Lucy gazed around. Seeing who had assembled for their wedding drove home the fact that Kahlil was an immensely powerful figure in the world at large. And she was—

'The mother of my son,' Kahlil said, introducing Lucy to the Ambassador of Abadan.

Lucy reddened as the older man bowed low over her hand.

'It is an honour to meet you at last, Princess,' he said.

Lucy's shocked eyes flickered up to meet Kahlil's steady gaze. 'It is my pleasure to meet you, Ambassador,' she said, recovering fast. Both the fact that Kahlil had taken the trouble to introduce them and the use of her new title had taken her completely by surprise.

'I hope you will excuse me for a few moments,' Kahlil said.

Gladly, Lucy thought, as he led the Ambassador away.

She needed time to collect her thoughts, to accept that, however short their marriage would be, her life had changed for ever. She watched as people gave way at Kahlil's approach, bowing low as he walked amongst them, and felt sure she would never get used to the fact that Sheikh Kahlil of Abadan was her husband.

Left to her own devices, Lucy began to relax and enjoy the celebrations. There were interesting new people to talk to, as well as many of her close friends and family. Skirting the subject of her new husband was something she was becoming rather good at, and after a while she began to believe that she would sail through the rest of the reception. It was a chance conversation that brought the idyll to an end.

'To think the Hall is to be a private home again. And after all these years.'

'I'm sorry?' Lucy said, collecting her thoughts. The Lady Mayor of Westbury had come to sit with her, and had been chattering non-stop for almost twenty minutes. 'I beg your pardon,' Lucy said, mending her manners. 'You were trying to tell me something about the Hall?'

'You must be so proud of your husband,' the Lady Mayor said, staring across the newly renovated ballroom at Kahlil, who was chatting easily as he moved around their guests.

'I am proud,' Lucy said automatically.

'He cuts a splendid figure in his tail-coat—and I imagine he would in Arabian garb. Still, I mustn't carp, or show my disappointment—his mother was English, after all.'

'I don't mean to interrupt,' Lucy said, desperate to halt the irrepressible flow of words from the older woman as concern brought questions leaping into her mind, 'but I thought the Hall was to be a hotel?'

'So did we all, my dear—until this morning. But now we hear different. And in my case,' she added proudly, 'from your husband himself. There are so many servants,' she breathed, turning around, oblivious to Lucy's shocked re-action. 'Still, what do you expect when a sheikh chooses to make his home in our village? To think,' she added, folding her hands as if in a prayer as she closed her eyes, 'that we are to have *royalty* living amongst us.'

Lucy felt as if all the life had just drained out of her. She fixed a smile to her lips, nodding politely. Kahlil had bought the Hall for his own use! Surely the Lady Mayor was mis-taken?

Lucy burned with shame as she remembered her surprise and relief when she had managed to sell the Hall for well over its market price—to a consortium of businessmen, the agent had said. Now she realised it had been Kahlil's way of paying her off. He had been behind the purchase all along, paying well over the odds—to appease his con-science? she wondered, remembering how abruptly he had left her after their one-night stand. She could just imag-ine his shock when he discovered she had given birth to Edward!

This marriage had been forced on him, Lucy thought, going cold as she surveyed the glittering scene. It put the gloss of respectability on his unfortunate mistake. But Sheikh Kahlil could afford it. For a man as rich as the Crown Prince of Abadan this was a bargain. For the price of a wedding he got the heir he longed for, with a wife to use while it pleased him thrown in.

'Well, I've kept you from your gorgeous husband long enough,' the Lady Mayor said, oblivious to Lucy's pain as she fluttered her chiffon handkerchief at a friend across the dance floor. 'I must let you go to him—I wish you every happiness, my dear,' she gushed, leaning over Lucy to plant a damp kiss on her cheek.

'Thank you,' Lucy said, her gaze hardening as she stared at Kahlil. Taking up her challenge, he came striding back to her, taking the direct route across the crowded dance floor. Once again Lucy noticed how a path cleared automatically in front of him.

'Lucy?'

His voice was sharp—with concern or irritation? She couldn't tell.

'Lucy, what is it? What's wrong?'

'I must speak to you,' she said, collecting the folds of her gown as she made to get up.

'Of course,' Kahlil said easily, suspecting nothing as he reached for a chair.

'Somewhere private,' Lucy stressed tensely, standing up.

'Very well,' he agreed, glancing round. 'I doubt anyone will notice that we've gone. Let me help you.'

She had no option but to take his arm—and Kahlil was probably right about no one noticing their departure, Lucy thought as they walked towards the doors. Their guests could not have been happier, or more content. It was ironic that only the bride and groom were so violently at odds with each other.

CHAPTER THIRTEEN

THE double height hall, with its sweeping staircase and min-strels' gallery, was quiet after the noise of the band and champagne-fuelled chatter.

But not quiet enough, not private enough, Lucy thought, leading the way, confident that she knew Westbury Hall better than anyone else. She drew to a halt outside one of the many doors leading off the hallway. But she didn't know which to go through now, she realised. Resting the palm of one hand against the cool, flat surface, she forced herself to accept that Westbury Hall now belonged to a stranger—and that stranger was her husband.

'Here,' Kahlil said, cupping her elbow and leading Lucy towards another door. 'We can be private in here.'

Lucy allowed him to steer her into the brightest room in the house—the room the previous owner, Lady Grace, had called her morning room. 'The room where all the problems are solved,' Lucy remembered Aunt Grace saying now. She blinked back tears, almost imagining she could hear the kindly old voice again, encouraging her to look round.

'You've kept everything the same,' she said with surprise, touching a blue silk cushion reverently.

'Those are new covers,' Kahlil admitted, 'but they are faithful copies of the originals. I thought it would be what you wanted.' He stayed by the door, watching her. 'Even before you mentioned Lady Grace Frobisher I'd heard you were very fond of her.'

But Lucy wasn't listening. 'It's all the same,' she exclaimed softly. 'Even down to the china dogs in the fire-place.' Dipping down, she stroked one smooth head.

'I was having them restored—there was a chip—but then I stopped.'

'You stopped?' she said, turning her face up to look at Kahlil.

'Some things can be spoiled by restoration,' he said. 'Sometimes their charm lies in the fact that many people have handled them, have enjoyed them over the years.'

As their eyes met and locked Lucy's were troubled. Kahlil understood so many things instinctively. And yet there were so many other matters that seemed to bypass him completely. Did he have no conscience at all? He could be sensitive, and about important things, like the keepsakes she treasured, but he withheld so much—too much. 'Why didn't you tell me about all this?' she said, straightening up to face him.

'We could hardly get married at your cottage, with a bodyguard in the spare room. I had Westbury Hall restored. I thought it a suitable venue for our wedding.'

'A suitable venue?' Lucy repeated, feeling the chance she had given him had just been wasted. 'So—' she gestured around '—all this is just for prestige? For the sake of how other people see you?'

'Not at all—'

'Tell me one thing. Were you behind the bank calling in my loan? Did you make them do that?'

Kahlil looked at her, his expression unreadable. 'It was a matter of business.'

'You deceived me, Kahlil,' she told him bitterly. 'You lied to me. You stole my dreams. And then you paid over the odds for Westbury Hall and allowed me to believe I had done a good deal—when in fact I was being paid for my services like a—'

'Don't speak that way!' Kahlil's voice cut across Lucy like a whip-crack. In an instant he had grabbed her arm in one powerful fist, and, cupping her chin with the other hand, he tilted Lucy's face until she couldn't avoid looking at him. 'Don't you even think like that,' he warned. 'You are the mother of my son. You are my wife. You have just become Princess of Abadan. Don't forget it.'

'I doubt I shall ever be allowed to forget it.' Lucy averted her face from Kahlil's blazing stare. 'Let me go, Kahlil,' she said faintly. 'Let me go now. We've got nothing more to say to each other.'

'Very well,' he agreed. 'Go to your room. I will make whatever excuses are necessary to our guests.'

With an angry sound, Lucy dragged her arm out of his clasp. But then she stopped on her flight to the door. 'I don't know which is to be my room.'

'All of them,' Kahlil said steadily.

'All of them?' Lucy said, turning to face him. 'What are you talking about?'

'I bought the Hall for my own reasons, but when I came to know you better I wanted you to have it. I did all this for you, Lucy,' Kahlil said in a bitter whisper. 'I thought it would make you happy. Don't worry,' he added, backing away when she reached towards him. 'I will have one of the servants show you to a suitable bedroom. You need have no fear. I won't trouble you tonight.'

The flight to Abadan was tense and lonely for Lucy. She was sitting in the main body of the aircraft, whilst Leila had taken Edward to sleep in a private suite at the rear.

Putting down the glossy magazine she had been pretending interest in for the past hour, Lucy gazed across at Kahlil and his ministers, clustered around a meeting table at the other side of the cabin. Things had gone from bad to worse since their wedding. She couldn't believe Kahlil had cheated her out of Westbury Hall, or that he'd meant to give the Hall back to her as a wedding present. Never in her wildest dreams could she have conceived of a gift on such a scale.

In her world wedding presents were toasters, or crystal glasses.

And now he was oblivious to her presence. Perhaps it was better that way. She would go and see if Edward was awake—

'Edward is sleeping; let him rest,' Kahlil said, without troubling to look at her. 'I will have lunch served here for us in a few moments.'

His uncanny knack of anticipating her intentions sent a frisson of alarm through Lucy. 'How do you know?'

'How do I know?' Kahlil repeated, turning a stare on her face.

'How do you know that Edward is still sleeping?'

Now she saw the monitor on the table in front of him. When he turned it towards her she realised the camera was trained on Edward's sleeping form. Next to Edward she could see Leila, sitting on an easy-chair, sewing a button onto a romper suit.

Security even on the royal jet, Lucy thought tensely, taking her seat again. And then she reddened, remembering the furious row she'd had with Kahlil that morning about security. She hadn't slept for one moment during her wedding night, and the last thing she had been expecting was that Kahlil would join her in the breakfast room.

She had started out wanting to apologise, to provoke a discussion at least. But Kahlil had rebuffed her. He'd preferred to eat in silence. Venting her frustration, she had complained about the high levels of security surrounding Edward, saying she feared they would intimidate him as he grew older and more aware.

'My son will not be intimidated by anything,' Kahlil had told her, stabbing a piece of omelette with his fork. 'It's time to grow up, Lucy,' he'd snapped then, throwing down his cutlery as he stared at her. 'Privilege has its price.'

Standing up, he'd thrust his chair back so violently it had made an angry, grinding noise on the wooden floor.

And then Leila had walked in, and Lucy had asked her to take Edward into the nursery for his breakfast rather than subject him to his parents' bickering. But Kahlil had walked out soon after that, brushing off her attempts to thank him for his wonderful gift. It was too late for thanks, he'd informed her coldly. And now Lucy felt as if she had never deserved to own the Hall in the first place...

Glancing down at the gold band on the third finger of her left hand, she saw how shiny it was—shiny and new and undamaged. Unlike her relationship with her husband of just a few hours. She had spent most of the flight working out how many contracts she would have to win to pay Kahlil back—for she *would* pay him back. She had made that promise to herself this morning. The gift of Westbury Hall was far too great. And after their non-existent wedding night she felt more determined than ever not to be in his debt.

She looked away as Kahlil flashed a glance at her. He looked unusually strained. She suspected the long celibate night had got to him every bit as much as it had got to her. If there was one thing that always went right between them it was sex. But there could have been so much more than that—if only Kahlil hadn't been so proud, and she hadn't been so defensive, so blinkered...

'Lucy?'

'Yes?' Lucy looked up as Kahlil moved to sit across from her.

'Is something wrong? I heard you sigh.'

'Nothing,' Lucy said quickly, dismissively. 'It was nothing. I was just daydreaming.'

'Then it is time you came to grips with reality,' he observed dryly, making a signal to the flight attendant.

Kahlil's concern was nothing more than the concern of a responsible employer for a member of staff, Lucy thought as she listened to him giving instructions to the flight attendant for lunch in the same low tone. And perhaps she could learn something from him; perhaps the six-month marriage would pass more easily if they learned to act politely but unemotionally towards each other.

'My wife and I will take lunch here,' he was saying. 'Everyone else will eat in the second compartment.'

The man bowed and went about his duties, leaving them alone. And then Lucy saw the Council members gathering up their papers as they prepared to move to another section of the plane.

'To us,' Kahlil murmured sardonically, raising a glass of chilled champagne.

Holding his gaze, Lucy took a sip. 'To us,' she repeated mechanically.

Putting his glass down on the table again, Kahlil looked at her. 'I have just finished dealing with a whole raft of problems, both large and small, troubling my employees. Would it help if I added yours to the mix?'

'No, it would not help,' Lucy said tensely. She was almost ready to accept the situation, but she wasn't in the mood for his irony. 'And as far as I am aware,' she added, 'I am no longer one of your employees. I am your wife.'

'Really?' Kahlil said, tilting his head to look at her. 'Not yet, you're not.'

Lucy gasped at his bluntness, and in the same instant felt the familiar tug of desire.

'And does your contract at the Golden Palace mean nothing to you?'

The contract! Lucy realised she hadn't even given it a thought...and there had been one or two minor complications that meant it might take longer than six months. 'Kahlil, we need to talk,' she said, putting down her glass.

'Yes, we do,' he agreed, crossing one lean denim-clad leg

easily over the other and keeping his dark, watchful eyes trained on her face.

'You know I have always intended to finish my work at the Golden Palace.' With no effort at all, Kahlil had put her on the defensive again. But he gave a small nod of his head, encouraging her to continue. 'And I will complete the contract,' she said. 'But I want neither your money nor your pity.'

'Who said you could have either?'

His eyes were narrowed, his firm, sensuous mouth curved in a cynical smile. He was playing her like a mouse, Lucy suspected. 'I just don't need a replay of Westbury Hall.'

'Explain,' Kahlil said, opening his hands.

'I want to complete my contract on the Golden Palace without your interference. The recovery of my business, the payment of my debts—everything I thought I had achieved through my own efforts—was only made possible because of you, because of your over-generous payment for Westbury Hall.'

'You built up your business before we met a second time,' he argued. 'I think you underestimate yourself.'

'I don't think so.'

'And as for the Hall—I paid what I thought it was worth.'

'And now you're giving it to me?'

'Yes.'

Lucy realised she had never felt so bad about anything. But was the Hall a gift or a pay-off, a bribe for six months' good behaviour? Her thoughts started flying in all directions.

'Was buying the Hall at an inflated price your way of paying me off?'

'Be under no illusion, Lucy. I have never had to pay for sex in my life.'

She believed him, and for a moment all she was aware of was Kahlil's eyes searching her own.

'Is that it?' he said, breaking eye contact at last. 'Or is there anything else you'd like to ask me?'

Or any insults she'd like to fling at him? he seemed to imply. But what more could she say? He had deceived her over Westbury Hall, and she had made no attempt to track down Edward's father. They were both in the wrong. Neither of them could deny what they had done.

The tension between them lifted a little when the flight attendant returned with a platter of salad. Lucy knew she could either fight with Kahlil for six months, or she could try and reach some sort of accommodation with him. But in order to reach a compromise she had to state her terms clearly.

'While we are married I will continue to work—'

'You'll certainly finish your contract,' he said dryly, looking up from his fork at her through a fringe of black lashes.

'Of course I will.'

'And as for Westbury Hall—don't talk about overpayment as if it is a crime. I may have behaved clumsily, but I was pleased to pay over the odds in order to ensure you did not suffer any more financial embarrassment. I wanted you to have the chance to get back on your feet—although you surpassed even my optimistic hopes for you by winning the design competition. No one was more surprised than me to see you in Abadan with a baby in tow.'

'Our baby.'

'Our baby,' he granted. 'My son.'

'Our son.'

Lucy gasped as Kahlil took hold of her upper arms in strong hands, and drew her to her feet in front of him.

'It is time to stop playing games, Lucy,' he said tensely. 'You're my wife now.'

Desire flared between them, but Lucy was still haunted by the memory of a man called Kahl: a man who had taken his fill and then taken his leave without a single word of explanation. She was determined to hold on to her self-control.

'So you get it all?' she said coolly, meeting Kahlil's gaze.

'Yes, I do,' he agreed. 'I get my son, I get Westbury Hall, and I get a wife—quite a haul, don't you think?'

His arrogance was breathtaking. Who did Kahlil think he was? A pirate? A buccaneer who seized everything in his path that pleased him? 'You haven't got me yet,' Lucy said with defiance, but the look in Kahlil's eyes had changed subtly in a way that made her want to melt against him.

'And you haven't received your wedding present yet,' he whispered, holding her so she couldn't get away.

'You gave me Westbury Hall—I don't want anything else.'

'You don't want anything else?' he repeated harshly. 'Forgive me if I disagree, but I think you do.'

Propelling her in front of him, Kahlil steered Lucy in the direction of his private quarters on board the royal jet.

CHAPTER FOURTEEN

THERE was a bed, a desk, and a sofa in Kahlil's spacious private cabin.

'Why have you brought me here?' Lucy said, wishing there was some alternative to staring him in the face. But he had her pinned against the door, with one arm resting at the side of her head, and was quite happy to let the moment hang.

The electricity between them was incredible, and Lucy suspected Kahlil enjoyed watching her suffer. It pleased him to look at her this way, watching her cheeks grow red with desire and her eyes darken with passion. She wanted him. She ached for him. Her whole body was on fire. She wished life could be simple! If it was Edward's happily married parents would on their way back with him now to a glowing future in Abadan. Instead of which—

'Why do you think we are here?' Kahlil's thoughts cut into hers like a knife. And then, before she could reply, he said, 'I've given you everything you asked for. Isn't it time you gave me something in return?'

Lucy went cold. All her passion subsided. She was his wife, and she had agreed to six months of married life to establish Edward's legitimacy. That was the price she had agreed to pay. But she had assumed it would be a marriage in name only, followed by a pain-free divorce. However much she wanted Kahlil, sex could never be something she made available on demand.

But she had misjudged him again, Lucy realised, as with one final assessing look Kahlil pulled away from her and walked across to the slim desk against the wall, where several documents were awaiting his attention in a pile.

'Come here,' he said, selecting one of them. 'You need to sign this.'

Lucy went to join him and, forced to lean over his shoulder, read the introduction. It was the contract she had never signed.

'You don't think a lot of me, do you, Lucy?' Kahlil said, swinging round to look at her.

On the contrary, Lucy thought. Her husband was an awe-inspiring individual by any measure. She would have been proud to acknowledge him as the father of her son without all the accoutrements of immense wealth, let alone the title he bore. Kahlil was exactly the type of man she would have chosen to father Edward. It was she who could never be a suitable wife for the future ruling Sheikh of Abadan.

'Pen?' he prompted. 'You should have signed this before the wedding and saved yourself a lot of unnecessary grief. I expect you haven't even read it through.'

Lucy couldn't meet his gaze.

'Just as I thought,' Kahlil said. 'You chose not to read it. You chose to think the worst of me.'

'A marriage contract seems so cold-blooded,' Lucy said honestly.

'Not in our case, surely? Did you expect romance?' he said when she didn't answer. 'Read it now,' he said, pulling out a chair for her to sit on.

Almost at once Lucy realised that the contract was weighted heavily in her favour. Her freedom from a loveless marriage was guaranteed after six months. She could even leave Kahlil sooner than that, should she choose to do so.

'No strings—no commitment,' he said, handing her a fountain pen.

The way Kahlil wanted it, she thought. 'Couldn't I have signed this out there?' she said, indicating the main cabin.

'Even my ministers do not know of our arrangement,' Kahlil said. 'It would undermine Edward's position if gossip spread.'

That made sense, Lucy conceded, signing the document. 'Thank you,' she said, returning the pen to Kahlil.

'You should feel reassured now,' he said, going to the door to open it for her.

She had been wrong about him all along, and now it was too late to make things right, Lucy realised. Her glance brushed the bed. The covers were pristine, untouched—and likely to remain that way for ever as far as she was concerned. Kahlil had given her everything she'd asked for and more: shared custody of Edward, freedom to continue working and providing for her son. Additions she hadn't even asked for included her own suite of rooms at the Golden Palace, and all the honour due to a princess of Abadan for the rest of her life. And he had given her the greatest gift of all: her freedom. But instead of feeling elated she felt beaten for the first time in her life.

'There is one more thing,' Kahlil said, picking up a bunch of keys from a table by the door. 'These belong to you now.'

The keys felt heavy and cold in Lucy's hands. 'Westbury Hall?' she murmured, staring down at them.

Kahlil inclined his head in assent.

Now she really did have everything she wanted, Lucy thought. And now she understood how little comfort bricks and mortar offered in place of the man she loved. 'Have you finished with me now?' she said faintly.

'Should there be more?' Kahlil said.

'No, of course not. I'll go and see Edward now.'

'Yes,' Kahlil said, making no move to follow her as Lucy returned to the main cabin. 'Go to your son.'

Late spring in Abadan had to be one of the most beautiful times of the year, Lucy thought as she sat on a ledge by the open window in her bedroom at the palace. And the silver dawn was definitely the most beautiful time of day.

Today was her wedding day—her Arabian wedding day. And this time she had no expectations, no false hopes. Kahlil had been as good as his word, leaving her to her own devices, not intruding on her work or her time with Edward. She should be satisfied. But instead she felt completely empty.

She was just starting to pull away from the window when something drew her back again. And then she saw Kahlil, dressed in riding breeches, striding across the courtyard flanked by his ministers. Time passed, but everything remained the same, Lucy mused, watching the same intense little man scurrying along by Kahlil's side, trying to keep up with him. Kahlil seemed to have a lot of instructions for him today, she noticed. But of course it was Kahlil's wedding day too—a thought so obvious, and yet incredible. He was like a stranger to her, a stranger she was about to marry—unless she took the initiative and changed the situation…

Impulsively, Lucy raced across the room to the ante-room where her clothes were kept. 'Where the hell…?' she muttered impatiently, slamming things back on the rails as she hunted for her jeans.

The royal stables were within easy walking distance of the main palace—the way Kahlil liked it. He could always clear his mind, think things through, relax and expend any excess energy he might be harbouring with a good gallop. And it was exactly what he needed now.

He had no idea how he was going to go through with it. The civil ceremony in England had been one thing—the dignitaries, the pomp and ceremony had meant nothing to him…not in his heart, not where it really mattered. But here, here in the vast burning truth of the desert, the simple ceremony in front of his people—people who trusted him, people who expected the best of him—

'Don't worry,' he said in Abadanese, when a groom hurried out to await his orders. 'I'll saddle him myself.'

He looked with pride at his stallion, Helix. The horse was perfectly proportioned, and hard, like a spring wound up to its limit. Just as he was, Kahlil reflected, slapping the flank of the magnificent black stallion to show his affection. The mighty creature nuzzled his shirt, hunting for the mints he kept there as he slipped a bridle over the proud head.

'He's beautiful.'

'Lucy!' Kahlil murmured in astonishment. And then, when his heart-rate had steadied a little, he added with concern, 'Shouldn't you be back at the palace, preparing yourself for the wedding? Several of our top beauticians have been brought in to wait on you.'

'Am I so ugly?'

The sudden humour threw him for a moment. 'No, no, of course you're not,' he said wryly.

'So I'm just vain?' Lucy suggested, playing along with him.

Kahlil shrugged as he tightened the girth. 'I thought you would like it—I thought they might help you to relax.'

'Could I ride with you?'

'Ride with me?' he said in astonishment. He hesitated with his hand on the saddle. It was the last thing on earth he had been expecting. 'Why not?' he murmured. And then he looked down the line of open stable doors, where several inquisitive heads were leaning out, ears pricked. 'A quiet gelding, perhaps?'

'What about this beautiful boy?'

'Helix? Don't be silly.'

'Silly?' Lucy queried, head on one side. 'Why, Kahlil? Is Helix a *man's* horse?'

'Well, yes…' Kahlil stopped. He could tell she was

teasing him. And he could see where it was leading. 'He's a very strong horse—hard to handle. Your physical strength—'

'Would not be equal to the task?' Lucy challenged, staring up at him steadily. 'I've seen your jockeys, Kahlil. They are all smaller than me.'

'And stronger.'

'How do you know that?'

They stared at each other head-on for a few seconds, then Kahlil spoke to the groom still hovering close by. 'Bring out Terco for me to ride.' And without another word he began to shorten the stirrups for Lucy, while the magnificent stallion snorted and raked the ground in anticipation of his morning gallop.

'Terco means *tough* in Spanish, doesn't it?' Lucy remarked, following Kahlil round. 'And *stubborn* is an alternative meaning, I believe. I think it's perfect that you should ride Terco,' she teased lightly when Kahlil had finished and turned to give her a look. 'But why does he have a Spanish name?'

'Because he is a Spanish horse,' Kahlil revealed, one corner of his mouth tugging up in the suspicion of a grin. 'My younger brother is a doctor. He lives in Spain. This horse was his wedding gift to me, and the name Terco is his idea of a joke. But you have chosen to ride my horse, Helix,' he reminded her. 'Changed your mind?'

'Certainly not.'

'Leg up?'

'Please,' Lucy said. She wasn't about to back down now. However terrifying the black stallion appeared as he struck sparks off the cobbles with his highly polished hooves, Kahlil needed to know she was equal to any challenge he might care to set.

The controlled pace they adopted to cross the immaculately clean stableyard gave no hint of the wild gallop to come. Kahlil increased speed slowly at first, as if he wanted to check out Lucy's riding ability, but once they reached the irresistible challenge of clear, flat scrubland he took off.

Determined not to be bettered, Lucy took his stallion to the limit. It was both the most terrifying and most exhilarating ride of her life. Leaning low over the horse's neck, she whispered encouragement into the horse's keenly pricked ears, and Helix didn't disappoint her. Lucy thrilled to the sound of his hooves thundering across the ground, and with his long nose stretched forward and his stride lengthening every moment he rewarded her encouragement with an easy win.

'You can certainly ride,' Kahlil admitted, when they drew level on a stretch of road and slowed the pace.

'Who couldn't ride with a horse like Helix beneath them?'

'Most people,' Kahlil told her dryly. 'But then most people wouldn't be brave enough to ride a horse like Helix in the first place.'

Praise? Lucy wondered, as Kahlil nudged Terco into a canter and took the lead.

She leaned back in the saddle as Kahlil led the way down a steep embankment, and then moved her weight forward to make it easier for the horse as he started up a steep, rocky hill. Stones skittered beneath the horses' hooves as they climbed up the narrow winding path, and then at last, when the path widened into a wide sandy arena, she saw the reason for their climb to the summit.

Far below them, spread out for miles across the desert, there were rows of neatly tethered camels and lines of trucks, and hordes of people milling about a vast, tented city.

'Our wedding guests,' Kahlil said, turning to look at her. 'Our people, Lucy.'

As the breeze lifted her hair into a curtain between them,

Lucy was glad of the moment's privacy. She was deeply moved, and intensely aware at the same time of the weight of responsibility she was about to take on. She was glad to share it with Kahlil, and saw the emotion in his gaze as he sat without speaking on Terco, lost in his own thoughts. It was certainly an awe-inspiring sight, and a huge challenge, but it was one she knew Kahlil embraced with humility and determination—just as she did.

They sat together quietly for quite a while, the two great horses at peace beneath them, as if the animals could sense the silent communion between their two riders more keenly than could Kahlil and Lucy.

It was as if they were all at one with the desert, Lucy reflected, breathing deeply on the warm, spicy air. The golden honeyed light, the chink of the horses' bridles as they lazily tossed their heads, the soft wind tugging at her hair… She gazed across at Kahlil, and at the same moment he turned too. And as they looked at each other Lucy exhaled slowly, feeling her whole body and spirit relax. She knew this stranger a little better now. It was as if something had passed between them. Not the fire of passion, the fire so fierce it had burned them both. This was something far deeper, and more lasting. She began to smile.

'We should be getting back,' Kahlil said, shortening the reins and turning Terco's head. 'Don't forget we are to be married today. We mustn't be late for our own wedding.'

'No,' Lucy agreed, taking one final look out over the desert encampment. And when she turned Helix and went to follow Kahlil down the stony path again his words were still echoing excitingly in her head: *We are to be married today…we are to be married today…we are to be married today…*

'That was quite a ride,' Kahlil called to her above the clatter of two sets of hooves rattling in tandem across the stableyard.

'It certainly was,' Lucy agreed, wiping her face on her sleeve.

'You're an accomplished horsewoman,' he added, making her glow with pleasure.

'You're not bad yourself.' In fact Kahlil was the most accomplished rider she had ever seen outside a show ring. And his stallion, Helix, had almost been too much for her—almost, but not quite. She had formed a pact with the mighty beast: he wouldn't throw her off and she would allow him to gallop flat out and keep his nose just ahead of Terco. Pride. It was just as important to every animal on the planet—both man and beast, Lucy reflected as she jumped down to the ground.

'Hey,' Kahlil exclaimed, just in time to catch her and prevent her falling to the ground when her legs gave way. 'Why didn't you wait for me to help you dismount?'

'Because I thought I was stronger than I am,' Lucy admitted, her legs still trembling violently after the exertions of the ride. But even if her limbs were letting her down, her spirit felt as if it had just had an injection of the great black stallion's energy. And this wasn't such a bad outcome, she conceded, relaxing into Kahlil's arms for a moment as the groom came to lead the horses away. 'That was a really great workout. Thank you,' she said, straightening up to face him.

'Thank you?' Kahlil said. 'There's no need for you to thank me, Lucy. These are as much your horses now as mine. And if I'd only known you rode so well we could have arranged to ride out together sooner.'

'That's just it, isn't it?' Lucy said quietly. 'We don't know anything about each other, do we, Kahlil?'

'We could learn.'

'Do you want to?'

He wasn't going to make it easy for her, Lucy realised

when Kahlil walked away from her without answering. She watched him carefully checking over the two horses for any unsuspected injuries now they were unsaddled.

'Sponge them down—they've had a good, hard run,' he said to the groom, shooting a faintly bemused glance at Lucy, as if he was still coming to terms with the fact that they might have something more in common than a son they both loved.

She could almost see him wondering what other surprises might lie in store…and she felt very much the same, Lucy realised as she turned to go.

'Wait.' Wiping his hands on his breeches, Kahlil came across to her. 'I just wanted to say—'

'Yes?' Lucy said, looking up at him.

'How much I enjoyed that,' Kahlil admitted, raking his fingers through his thick black hair as if he was unused to making such declarations.

Lucy felt as if the air was a little clearer, the sky a little bluer, and her heart was suddenly far too big for her chest. 'So did I,' she said softly, staring deep into Kahlil's eyes.

'Lucy, is it too late?'

'Too late?' she said.

'For you to stay?'

'I won't leave until the six months are up,' she promised.

'I don't mean that. I mean—' Kahlil looked away from her, back towards the stables, where the horses were leaning over the half-open doors as if they too were keen to hear what he had to say. 'Will you stay longer than six months?' he said.

It was as if he found any admission of personal need awkward and embarrassing, Lucy realised. 'Do you think I should?' she asked.

'I think you must,' Kahlil said passionately.

'I must?'

'Please,' he said, 'don't accuse me of trying to control you again.' His voice was strained, and his eyes lingered on Lucy's lips as if he couldn't wait to kiss them again.

'I won't,' she promised, her own gaze straying to Kahlil's firm and very sensuous mouth.

'I want you to stay longer than six months.'

'How long, Kahlil?' Lucy said, searching his eyes.

'I want you to stay with me—for ever. I love you, Lucy.'

'You love me?' she repeated incredulously.

'I don't want you to leave me—I couldn't bear it if you left me,' Kahlil admitted. 'There is no one I would rather have to sit beside me one day on the throne of Abadan, no one else I want to bear my children, and no one but you can be my wife.'

Lucy could never have imagined Kahlil expressing himself in such an emotional way. The man she knew was all duty to his country, all fierce control over his life... 'Then I'll stay,' she said simply. And if he changed his mind when he had thought it through she would take him on any terms. She couldn't contemplate a future without Kahlil.

'You'll stay as my wife?'

'We are married. And we're to be married again in just a few hours.'

'I know marriage to me will be hard for you,' he said. 'I know you will have to embrace many responsibilities. It's hardly fair of me to ask you—'

Raising her hand, Lucy placed one finger over Kahlil's lips, silencing him. 'You want me to stay here in Abadan and be your wife? You know I will. We will be married for the next six months, and then, if you want me to stay on...'

Taking her hand away and unfolding it to kiss her palm, Kahlil raised his eyes. 'If you will have me, Lucy Benson, I want you to be my wife for a lot longer than six months.'

When Lucy couldn't speak he kissed her.

* * *

The wedding was to be held in the early evening, as tradition demanded in Abadan. So she had the rest of the day to prepare, Lucy thought, coming back into her bedroom after her shower. Edward was being well taken care of by Leila, who'd said she should have some quiet time by herself.

Right now, quiet time was the last thing she wanted, Lucy thought, securing a towel around her damp hair as she wandered across to the window. She wanted to jump up and down and share her happiness with everyone. She wanted to lean out of the window and shout out the news that Kahlil, Sheikh of Abadan, loved her.

Fastening her robe a little more securely, she planted her hands on the stone ledge and stared out. She smiled, picturing the usual early-morning group, with Kahlil at its head and his loyal aide bustling along next to him. And then her smile faltered. Was she making too much of it? Had the ride into the hills been just a fleeting, if rather wonderful moment? There was such a history of mistrust and misunderstanding between them—was one morning enough to set things right?

She wouldn't know the answer to that until after the wedding. Kahlil was far too concerned with fine-tuning the last-minute arrangements.

Leila had said that over a thousand wedding guests were expected—and that might even be a conservative estimate, Lucy thought, remembering the tented city Kahlil had shown her. Tribesmen were arriving from every corner of his desert kingdom for the ceremony. Her heart thundered with excitement at the thought of it.

Pulling away from the window, Lucy smiled to herself as she remembered every moment of Kahlil's kiss. It had been so tender; he had never kissed her like that before. And romance was in the air. Even the sternest of his attendants were smiling and singing under their breath, and the women insisted on scattering rose petals beneath her feet every chance they got.

But perhaps it would be better not to get carried away. Maybe Kahlil was just trying to be kind to her, to thank her in his own way for her co-operation... But something had definitely sparked into life between them during their hair-raising gallop across the desert. Something that had brought them closer than words—but then again maybe she was imagining the whole thing, Lucy thought with a sigh.

'That's a heart-felt sigh. I thought our ride had exorcised all your devils—apparently I was mistaken?'

'Kahlil!' He had just showered, Lucy realised. His hair was still damp and he was dressed in a simple Arab robe, his head covered with a flowing white *gutrah* that contrasted starkly against his tan. 'I didn't expect you.'

'So I see,' he said, coming closer. 'I believe we have some unfinished business. But before we get to that...'

'Yes?' Lucy said, feeling her buoyant mood dissolve and wondering why.

'There's something I have to say to you—something I have to tell you. No,' he said firmly, softly, 'don't turn away from me, Lucy. There have been too many misunderstandings between us, and I want to set things straight before we are married—truly married. Will you give me that chance?'

'Of course,' Lucy whispered, wanting to stop up her ears for fear of what he might say.

'My initial intention was to take Westbury Hall from you without a moment's conscience or hesitation.' Kahlil brought Lucy in front of him so she couldn't escape the harsh truth he had to tell her. 'I wanted the Hall for myself, for my new palace, and only you stood in my way. I forced the bank to withdraw your loan. I did cheat you. As for the purchase of the Hall being a game for me—you were right. It did start as a game—but it ended as a love match.'

'And that first time we made love?'

'I wanted you. I didn't plan to fall in love—just as you didn't know that Edward would bring us back together again. I had to tell you the truth, Lucy, before the ceremony. Can you forgive me?'

'Can you forgive me?' she said softly. 'For keeping Edward from you?'

Kahlil's answer was to trace the outline of Lucy's face very lightly with one hand. 'I can only thank you for bringing my son to me, and for coming back into my life,' he said, staring deep into her eyes.

'Won't it cause comment if we are seen together before the wedding?' Lucy said, reading Kahlil's gaze.

'We have no such superstitions here in Abadan,' he assured her in a whisper. 'And I have dismissed the servants...no one will disturb us.'

Lucy felt her legs weaken and sensuous heat flood her veins. 'We will be married tonight in the eyes of your countrymen...'

'Must I wait?' Kahlil demanded softly.

'Can you?'

'No,' he admitted wryly.

'No control?' Lucy whispered.

'No wish to wait—because I love you, Lucy Benson.'

And then he kissed her, backing her towards the bed, stripping off her towelling robe at the same time. The towel on Lucy's head tumbled to the floor seconds later, releasing her soft blonde hair so it tumbled around her shoulders in shimmering disarray. And when she lifted her arms to try and arrange it more neatly Kahlil wouldn't let her.

'That's how I like to see you,' he murmured. Running his fingertips lightly over the inside of her uplifted arms, he moved on to the round globes of her breasts, cupping them in his hands, weighing them appreciatively, his fingers straying to tantalise her painfully engorged nipples. 'Now...shall

I let you wait until our wedding night, or would you like me to continue?'

For answer Lucy spread her fingers over his shoulders and clutched him tight, her eyes imploring as she dragged him with her to the bed.

'Oh, well,' Kahlil said, laughing under his breath at her eagerness, 'if you insist...'

'I do,' Lucy assured him, raising her eyebrows as she lay back on the silken coverlet. 'But you're rather overdressed,' she chastised him softly, smiling approval when he stripped off his clothes.

'Now I'm not,' Kahlil said, stretching his naked length out beside her, barely touching, so that Lucy began to tingle all over her body, from the top of her head to the tip of her toes.

'Kahlil, don't tease me.'

'Why not?' he demanded softly, running the tips of his fingers down between her breasts and on over the soft swell of her stomach. 'It's what I do best, after all.'

With a groan, Lucy reached for him. She'd had enough teasing, enough waiting too. He was everything she wanted—everything she needed. And it had been far, far too long.

They fit together so completely, so perfectly, the pleasure was almost unendurable. Sinking deep inside her, Kahlil moved slowly, deeply, and then, when she thought that it was everything pleasure could be, and was grateful for it, he sank even deeper, and moved from side to side, nudging, pressing, rubbing until she cried out in ecstasy and couldn't wait for him to tip her over the edge.

'Restraint,' Kahlil warned softly, starting to move again when she quietened. 'Haven't I taught you the Eastern way?'

'The Western way isn't so bad,' Lucy whispered against

his mouth. 'My quantity, your quality—a perfect blend, wouldn't you agree?'

Kahlil's answer was a groan of pleasure equal to her own as she reached down and cupped him, running the tips of her sharp fingernails very lightly across the tautly stretched flesh beneath his pulsing erection. And then he turned her quickly, unexpectedly, so that she was mounted on top of him.

'I've seen you ride,' he reminded her, stroking her buttocks with the most tantalisingly light touch. 'So, ride…'

'We're going to be late for our own wedding,' Lucy warned Kahlil very much later. Stretching out one blush pink arm, she picked up her wristwatch.

Every part of her was blush-pink, she realised with amusement, falling back onto the bed beside Kahlil. His stamina was extraordinary.

'Thank goodness tonight is our wedding night,' she said, speaking her thoughts out loud. She could hardly wait until he made love to her again.

'And thank goodness it will be a very different wedding night from our first,' Kahlil murmured, reaching up to brush an errant strand of hair off Lucy's face. 'I don't think I could stand another night of cold sheets and inertia.

'You too?' she said, smiling.

'Me too,' Kahlil admitted wryly.

'OK, so I promise you hot sheets and constant action,' Lucy said, laughing as she fell into his arms. 'But right now, Sheikh Kahlil, we have to get up.'

Kahlil made a sound of agreement deep in his throat. 'More's the pity. I must take you riding again very soon.'

'I can't wait,' Lucy said happily. 'Only…'

'Only?' Kahlil said, pulling her back so he could look into her face.

'Do you have any quiet geldings in your stable?'

Throwing his head back, Kahlil laughed. 'It's your stable too now,' he reminded Lucy. 'You choose whichever horse you want. Were you frightened this morning?' he said, frowning a little.

'Terrified,' Lucy admitted, remembering Kahlil's fiery stallion.

'Why didn't you say something?'

'What—and have you think me a coward? No, thank you.'

'I would not have thought you a coward,' Kahlil assured her. 'Your courage has never been in question.'

'So a nice quiet gelding next time?' Lucy suggested hopefully.

'Whatever you want…whatever makes you happy. Whatever your heart desires I will give you.'

'Then that's easy,' she said, growing still. 'Because all I want, Kahlil, is you.'

There was a fever in her wedding preparations this time. Lucy checked and rechecked her appearance in the mirror umpteen times. She wasn't a beauty. She couldn't do much about that. But did she look good enough? The Eastern robes were concealing, but flattering, and played to her generous curves. The colour and the fabric Kahlil had chosen for her were amazing—softest pale blue silk chiffon covered in tiny glittering bugle beads and pearls.

'Do you like it?' Leila said, smiling at Lucy while balancing an awestruck Edward on her hip.

'Like it?' Lucy murmured, allowing the ice-blue gossamer fabric to float from her fingers. 'Who wouldn't love a gown like this, Leila? It's so beautiful. I can't believe it.'

'Don't forget your sandals.'

They were sprinkled with diamonds—she wasn't likely to overlook them, Lucy thought ruefully as she slipped them on. Would she ever become accustomed to such wealth? She doubted it.

'Do you like your own outfit?' she asked with concern.

Leila was becoming increasingly important to her; she was part of the family now as far as Lucy was concerned. And even though time had been so short Lucy had taken special care in selecting something she thought Leila might enjoy wearing. She was to be an attendant at the marriage ceremony with Edward. Both had outfits in a subtle blue a little deeper than her own dress colour, and their clothes were fastened with tiny sapphire buttons and beaded with creamy freshwater pearls.

'I like this the best of all,' Leila said, fingering the locket Lucy had given to her as a wedding-day present. 'You're really very kind.'

'And so are you. I couldn't do this without you. Team Benson—remember?'

'Team ben Saeed Al-Sharif of Abadan,' Leila reminded her, and as Edward clapped his hands together with excitement they all began to laugh.

Kahlil surprised them, striding across the room resplendent in his wedding robes.

Lucy was grateful to Leila for putting Edward down for a moment and quickly swinging a silk robe over her shoulders. She wanted Kahlil to see her in her wedding dress for the first time at their marriage ceremony.

'Thank you, Leila,' Kahlil said, when the girl, sensing something exciting was about to happen between the bride and groom, swept Edward into her arms and quickly left the room.

'Kahlil?' Lucy said when the door shut had quietly behind Leila. 'I didn't expect to see you before the wedding.'

'I have something for you,' he said, bringing her hand to his lips. Kissing each of her fingertips in turn, he turned her hand to kiss her palm. And then placing two rings in her hand he closed Lucy's fingers over them.

'For you,' Kahlil said softly, when she looked at him in confusion.

Opening her hand again, Lucy stared down at the rings.

'I chose the diamond ring for you as the mother of my son. Something for you to remember me by when the six months of our marriage were over.'

Lucy stared at the fabulous jewel in awe. But the second ring was quite different, and as the realisation of who must have worn it came over her Lucy drew in an astonished breath.

'This ring is for an unconventional wife and an unconventional marriage,' Kahlil murmured.

'Is it really Nurse Clemmy's ring?' Lucy whispered, hardly able to believe what Kahlil was offering her.

'Will you wear it?' Kahlil said, gazing at her steadily. 'Will you marry me, Lucy Benson? I should warn you that the woman who wears this ring will stay with me for ever, and work alongside me for the good of our people. It is a ring for the woman of the Sheikh's heart to wear.'

'Then it is the only ring I choose to wear,' Lucy told him.

Something fundamental had changed between the two of them, Lucy realised when she joined Kahlil beneath the bridal canopy. The electricity, the immediate surge of desire was as strong as ever, but now there was more. And it filled her with fear, and with joy, and hope, and with all the butterfly flutterings in her stomach that a bride should expect to feel on her wedding day.

Closing her eyes for a moment, before she gave her hand to Kahlil, Lucy inhaled the exotic scents of the flowers around her. As well as over the canopy, the women had bound flowers in her hair. Fragrant blossoms circled the translucent blue veil that matched her eyes exactly, and they had put a garland around her neck too, over the intricately embroidered robe she knew they had taken hours beading and embroidering. She felt beautiful, and feminine.

There was such a groundswell of love from the people of Abadan for Edward and for herself—a love Lucy returned wholeheartedly. And now there was complete balance in her relationship with Kahlil. She knew their future together was assured. Opening her eyes, she found Kahlil smiling at her, and it was with total confidence that she placed her hand in his.

'You look beautiful,' he whispered as a hush fell over the assembled congregation. Then, bringing her hand to his lips, he turned it over and placed the diamond-encrusted ring on her palm.

'What—?' Lucy looked at him in confusion.

'For six months only,' he teased her softly, 'and then, if you tire of it, I'll buy you another one.'

'Kahlil...' Lucy chastened him in a low voice.

Then he placed the thin, well-worn gold band on the third finger of her marriage hand. 'But this ring,' he said softly, 'is for the wife of my heart. This ring, my darling Lucy, is for ever.'

If you enjoyed what you just read,
then we've got an offer you can't resist!

Take 2 bestselling love stories FREE!

Plus get a FREE surprise gift!

Clip this page and mail it to Harlequin Reader Service®

IN U.S.A.
3010 Walden Ave.
P.O. Box 1867
Buffalo, N.Y. 14240-1867

IN CANADA
P.O. Box 609
Fort Erie, Ontario
L2A 5X3

YES! Please send me 2 free Harlequin Presents® novels and my free surprise gift. After receiving them, if I don't wish to receive anymore, I can return the shipping statement marked cancel. If I don't cancel, I will receive 6 brand-new novels every month, before they're available in stores! In the U.S.A., bill me at the bargain price of $3.80 plus 25¢ shipping & handling per book and applicable sales tax, if any*. In Canada, bill me at the bargain price of $4.47 plus 25¢ shipping & handling per book and applicable taxes**. That's the complete price and a savings of at least 10% off the cover prices—what a great deal! I understand that accepting the 2 free books and gift places me under no obligation ever to buy any books. I can always return a shipment and cancel at any time. Even if I never buy another book from Harlequin, the 2 free books and gift are mine to keep forever.

106 HDN DZ7Y
306 HDN DZ7Z

Name _____ (PLEASE PRINT)

Address _____ Apt.#

City _____ State/Prov. _____ Zip/Postal Code

Not valid to current Harlequin Presents® subscribers.

Want to try two free books from another series?
Call 1-800-873-8635 or visit www.morefreebooks.com.

* Terms and prices subject to change without notice. Sales tax applicable in N.Y.
** Canadian residents will be charged applicable provincial taxes and GST.
   All orders subject to approval. Offer limited to one per household.
   ® are registered trademarks owned and used by the trademark owner and or its licensee.

PRES04R   ©2004 Harlequin Enterprises Limited

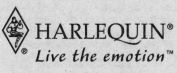

Coming Next Month

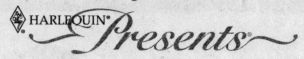

THE BEST HAS JUST GOTTEN BETTER!

#2487 THE RAMIREZ BRIDE Emma Darcy

Nick Ramirez has fame, fortune—and any girl he wants! But now he's forced to abandon his pursuit of pleasure to meet his long-lost brothers. He must find a wife and produce an heir within a year. And there's only one woman he'd choose to be the Ramirez bride....

#2488 EXPOSED: THE SHEIKH'S MISTRESS Sharon Kendrick

As the ruler of a desert kingdom, Sheikh Hashim Al Aswad must marry a respectable woman. He previously left Sienna Baker when her past was exposed—and he saw the photos to prove it! But with passion this hot, can he keep away from her...?

#2489 THE TYCOON'S TROPHY WIFE Miranda Lee

Reece knew Alanna would make the perfect trophy wife! Stunning and sophisticated, she wanted a marriage of convenience. But suddenly their life together was turned upside down when Reece discovered that his wife had a dark past....

#2490 AT THE FRENCH BARON'S BIDDING Fiona Hood-Stewart

When Natasha de Saugure was summoned to France by her grandmother, inheriting a grand estate was the last thing on her mind—but her powerful new neighbor, Baron Raoul d'Argentan, believed otherwise. His family had been feuding with Natasha's for centuries—and the Baron didn't forgive....

#2491 THE ITALIAN'S MARRIAGE DEMAND Diana Hamilton

Millionaire Ettore Severini was ready to marry until he learned that Sophie Lang was a scheming thief! Now when he sees her again, Sophie is living in poverty with a baby.... Ettore has never managed to forget her, and marriage will bring him his son, revenge and Sophie at his mercy!

#2492 THE TWELVE-MONTH MISTRESS Kate Walker

Joaquin Alcolar has a rule—never to keep a mistress for more than a year! Cassie's time is nearly up.... But then an accident leaves Joaquin with amnesia. Does this mean Cassie is back where she started—in Joaquin's bed, with the clock started once more...?

HPCNM0805